COLTON'S DEEP COVER

BY
ELLE KENNEDY

MILLS &
BOON

First published in Great Britain 2013
by Mills & Boon, an imprint of Harlequin (UK) Limited,
Eton House, 18-24 Paradise Road, Richmond, Surrey TW9 1SR

© Harlequin Books S.A. 2012

Special thanks and acknowledgement to Elle Kennedy for her contribution to The Coltons of Eden Falls miniseries.

ISBN: 978 0 263 90351 5
ebook ISBN: 978 1 472 00705 6

46-0313

Harlequin (UK) policy is to use papers that are natural, renewable and recyclable products and made from wood grown in sustainable forests. The logging and manufacturing processes conform to the legal environmental regulations of the country of origin.

Printed and bound in Spain
by Blackprint CPI, Barcelona

A RITA® Award-nominated author, **Elle Kennedy** grew up in the suburbs of Toronto, Ontario, and holds a BA in English from York University. From an early age she knew she wanted to be a writer, and actively began pursuing that dream when she was a teenager. She loves strong heroines and sexy alpha heroes, and just enough heat and danger to keep things interesting.

Elle loves to hear from her readers. Visit her website, www.ellekennedy.com, for the latest news or to send her a note.

To Justine Davis, Beth Cornelison
and Marie Ferrarella—
I'm honored to be in such amazingly talented company!

Chapter 1

"I need to see you in my office, Amelia."

Chloe Moreno froze as her boss's soft-spoken request sounded from behind. She'd been in the process of pulling a patient chart from the large steel cabinet in the file room, but now her fingers trembled, causing her to lose her grip on the Danford file. It fluttered to the shiny linoleum floor, and as papers spilled out of the blue folder, the heat of embarrassment blasted through her.

Cheeks scorching, Chloe dropped to her knees and quickly collected the strewn papers. "Sorry. I'm such a klutz some-times," she murmured, keeping her eyes downcast. "Let me just pick this up and I'll meet you in your offi—"

A shadow fell over her. Clothing rustled as her boss knelt down, his big, gorgeous hands reaching out to help her collect the papers.

Swallowing, Chloe gathered up the courage to lift her head—and found a pair of deep brown eyes watching her in amusement.

"No need to look so terrified," Derek Colton said in that smooth, baritone voice of his. "I'm not going to fire you for dropping a file, Amelia."

Amelia. Lord, would she ever get used to that name? It was the reason she'd dropped the file in the first place; hearing

Derek address her by a name that wasn't her own made her so damn uneasy, so very jittery.

You're Amelia Phillips now. Get used to it.

Chloe drew in a breath, heeding the commanding voice in her head. She couldn't keep jumping at shadows and battling a sense of disorientation each time someone called her Amelia. She was Amelia. Chloe Moreno was dead. And according to the *LA Times* website, Felix had shelled out the big bucks for her memorial service. A funeral hadn't been an option, seeing as her body was presumed to be at the bottom of the Pacific.

Shoving the unwelcome thoughts from her mind, Chloe rose to her feet and tucked the patient file under her arm. Derek stood up, too, his six-foot frame towering over her.

A shiver danced up her spine, a common occurrence in this man's presence. Derek Colton was too attractive for his own good—tall, muscular, ruggedly handsome. And his chocolate-brown eyes were too damn perceptive. Each time he focused that intense gaze on her, she felt as if he was peering into her soul. Like he knew all her secrets.

But he didn't. He couldn't. Chloe herself had lost track of all the secrets and lies. Over the past six months she'd spun a web so thickly complex that she didn't even know who she was anymore.

She knew who she *wasn't,* though.

Chloe, the wife of celebrity plastic surgeon Felix Moreno, no longer existed. She'd been replaced with Amelia, the quiet, hardworking nurse who'd impressed the heck out of her new boss when she'd helped him save a patient from bleeding out three weeks ago.

And as long as she continued to impress Derek with her skills, she could stay in Eden Falls and live the life she'd always dreamed of.

The life she'd *earned.*

So, pasting on a professional smile, she glanced at Derek and said, "What did you need to talk about?"

"Let's go to my office." His expression revealed nothing, no hint of what he needed to discuss with her.

As Chloe trailed after him, she took a calming breath, silently praying that he wasn't about to fire her. Unfortunately, inhaling was a bad idea because it only succeeded in drawing Derek's appealing scent into her lungs. The man smelled so good, like soap and aftershave and something intoxicatingly masculine.

Her gaze homed in on his broad back, covered by the white coat that contrasted with his smooth, mocha skin. He kept his black hair in a buzz cut, which left the nape of his strong, corded neck exposed. Another shiver ran through her as she admired him, and she was grateful that he couldn't see her face. She'd worked hard to hide her visceral reaction to this man, the flames that licked at her flesh each time he flashed one of those sexy, easygoing smiles in her direction.

Derek led her down the brightly lit hallway of the clinic. When they reached his office, he opened the door and gestured for her to enter first, just like the gentleman he was. Gosh, she'd never met anyone like him—the man oozed charm and sex appeal, yet at the same time, he exuded a quiet strength that was downright inspiring.

In the three weeks she'd worked as a nurse in Derek's practice, she'd been so tempted to dig deeper and get to know this intriguing man, but the need to maintain a certain level of professionalism had reined in the impulse. This job meant everything to her. Getting chummy with the boss would be a bad idea, especially because she hadn't exactly told him the truth about who she really was.

"Have a seat," Derek said pleasantly, gesturing to one of the plush chairs in front of his commanding mahogany desk.

Chloe sat, nervously crossing her ankles.

Derek settled in his leather chair and clasped his hands. "I wanted to discuss your performance," he began, those deep brown eyes seeking her out again.

She experienced a twinge of panic. "Oh. Did I do something wrong?"

He chuckled, and the husky sound teased her senses. "On the contrary. You're doing everything right. I wanted to talk about making this arrangement permanent."

Relief and pleasure washed over her. "Really?"

"Really," he said with a twinkle in his eyes. "I know we didn't have a chance to talk about the long term, what with you being thrust into this practice so abruptly. Have I told you how wonderfully you handled the Violet Chastain situation?"

Fighting a burst of pride, Chloe smiled. "Numerous times. How is Violet doing, by the way?"

"Nearly fully recovered and driving my brother crazy." Derek grinned. "But he loves it. I don't think I've ever seen Gunnar this happy."

Yeah, love could do that to a person. Or so she'd heard. Chloe hadn't lucked out in the relationship department, unlike Derek's older brother Gunnar, who'd found happiness with Hollywood starlet Violet Chastain. Violet had been in town researching a movie role when she'd been attacked and left for dead on the side of the road. Fortunately, she'd survived the assault and near-kidnapping and found a loving partner in Gunnar Colton, who'd stepped in to help Violet with her twin boys while she recovered from the injury to her leg.

Although Violet had gotten her happy ending, managing to escape her assailants, the attackers had abducted the young woman who'd been accompanying the actress.

The memory brought an ache to Chloe's heart. "Has there been any word on Mary and Hannah?"

Derek instantly sobered. "None. Emma and Tate are still working the case, but there are no new leads."

She shook her head in dismay, unable to comprehend the events that had transpired. The town of Eden Falls bordered Paradise Ridge, which was home to a small Amish community looking to live quiet, peaceful lives. But there was nothing peaceful about recent events. Four Amish girls had disappeared over the past month. Two had been found dead in a remote cabin near the Colton ranch, and the other two—Mary Yoder and Hannah Troyer—were still missing.

Derek's siblings, Emma and Tate, both worked in law enforcement, and while investigating the disappearances, they'd uncovered a horrific truth—the missing girls were being sold in a sex ring that catered to seedy buyers with even seedier intentions. Emma had gotten closer to Hannah's brother Caleb over the course of the investigation.

It sounded unimaginable, yet it didn't surprise Chloe to learn that sadistic people like that existed.

After all, she'd spent the past twelve years living with her very own personal sadist.

"I hate thinking about what those girls must be going through," Derek said. His handsome face revealed the frustration he felt over the situation. "I wish I could do more to help, but I fear I'd only get in Emma and Tate's way."

"I wish I could do more, too," she said softly, her heart breaking for those missing girls.

"Well, you're doing your fair share around here," Derek answered, steering the discussion back on track. "I'm going to be honest, Amelia. You're a real asset to this clinic. Having you around these past few weeks has made me realize I can't afford to lose you. That's why I wanted to sit down with you and talk about your plans."

"My plans?" Chloe echoed.

He nodded. "I wanted to make sure you still plan on making Eden Falls your home, that you're not going to suddenly pack your bags and move to Philly or accept a job with some other big-city hospital."

"Not at all," she blurted out. "Eden Falls is where I want to be, Dr. Colton. And the only job I'm interested in is this one."

"That's good to hear." Those brown eyes danced playfully. "And how many times must I remind you to call me Derek?"

"Right. Sorry. D-Derek." Her voice wobbled, and she tried not to cringe. She was forty-one years old, for crying out loud. Why did she always stammer like a schoolgirl in the presence of this man?

Derek seemed to be fighting a grin, which told her he'd picked up on her bout of nervousness. "Well, if you're serious about sticking around, then I want you to know I'm thrilled to have you. It still amazes me at times, the calming effect you have on anyone you come into contact with." He looked vaguely embarrassed. "You're really good with the patients, Amelia."

"So are you." The abrupt admission caused her cheeks to heat up again.

Uh, suck up much?

Fine, she had a total case of hero-worship when it came to Derek Colton. But how could she not? The man happened to be an incredible doctor. He had an easy rapport with his patients, and he carried himself with a self-assuredness that made her envious. She wished she had half the confidence that this talented doctor possessed in spades.

Also, it didn't hurt that he was drop-dead gorgeous, which meant that taking orders from him could hardly be considered a chore. And even though she had about ten years on him, he carried himself with a sense of maturity and strength that tugged at something inside her. Derek was a first-class man, the kind of man she wouldn't have believed existed if she hadn't just spent three weeks by his side.

"Anyway, that was all I wanted," Derek said, scraping back his chair. "Could you prepare the exam room for our three o'clock?"

"Of course." Chloe stood and smoothed out the hem of her shirt. "I already pulled up the Danford file."

A smile tugged on the corners of his mouth. "Efficient as always, aren't you, Amelia?"

"Just trying to make an impression on the boss," she answered lightly.

He chuckled again.

Her heart did a little flip.

Oh, brother. This had to stop. Her growing attraction to Derek was becoming a total nuisance. She hadn't traveled clear across the country to get lovesick about a man.

She was still a married woman, after all.

As a lump of bitterness rose in her throat, Chloe quickly banished the reminder. "I'll prep the exam room," she said before ducking out of Derek's office.

Her white sneakers squeaked against the floor as she hurried down the hall. She sucked in a few deep breaths, wishing she could erase the memory of Felix from her mind. But each time she thought she was close to forgetting her former life, those annoying reminders crept in like a cat burglar.

Why couldn't she just put the past behind her? After too many years of living in fear and being tormented by the man she'd foolishly married, she was finally free of Felix Moreno. She'd spent the past two years painstakingly preparing for this, stashing money, renewing her nursing license, arranging her escape. Once she'd gotten free, she'd spent six months making her way east, never staying in one place for long while she waited for the dust to settle. Waited until she could be absolutely certain that Felix truly believed she was dead.

She'd wound up in Eden Falls, Pennsylvania, by pure chance—she'd run out of gas right outside of town. She'd intended on filling the tank and continuing on to Philadelphia, but the moment she'd laid eyes on the idyllic Eden Falls, she'd fallen in love. This small town had everything she'd always dreamed of and never had in California—warmth, joy, a tight-knit sense of family and community. There was nothing fake about the people of Eden Falls; they were kind, decent folks who looked out for each other, which was the complete opposite of the phony, materialistic people she'd been surrounded with her entire life.

When she'd sat in the little diner in the heart of downtown and flipped through the newspaper, the job ad she'd come across had been like a neon sign from a higher power. The clinic in town was in need of a nurse—and what do you know, Chloe had a nursing degree just waiting to be put to use again.

This past month had been so utterly wonderful. She loved her job, adored her cozy one-bedroom apartment, respected the heck out of her boss.

So why was she still battling the impulse to continually look over her shoulder?

As Chloe entered the exam room, something cold touched her cheek. She jumped, then relaxed when she realized it was her own hand. She'd involuntarily begun to stroke the left side of her face, a nervous gesture she'd been trying to wean herself out of. She didn't want to draw any undue attention to her face, and besides, the thin ridge of scar tissue marring her skin beneath the makeup simply served as another reminder of the life she'd left behind.

Letting her hand drop, she crossed the room and quickly rolled a fresh sheet of exam paper over the table. Then she strode toward the cabinet against the far wall and removed a blue hospital johnny.

As she placed the gown on the table, she squared her shoulders, forcing her brain into work mode. She couldn't agonize over Felix anymore. She was free now. Safe.

And happy. Damn it, for the first time in her life she was honest-to-God happy, and she refused to let Felix Moreno take that away. He'd already taken too much from her. He'd terrorized her, scarred her, humiliated her.

But he hadn't broken her.

As a rush of pride welled up in her belly, Chloe left the exam room and headed for the waiting area, banishing all thoughts of Felix and her past from her mind. The only thing she needed to focus on right now was calling in the next patient and proving to Derek Colton that hiring her had been the best decision he'd ever made.

Had he made the wrong decision in hiring Amelia?

Derek puckered his brows as he watched his new nurse slip her arm through Rachel Danford's. He couldn't hear what Amelia was saying, but he made out the encouraging note in her soft voice.

Rachel and her husband, Jacob, looked stricken as they listened to Amelia. Jacob was strong and stoic in his dark trousers, brown suspenders and white shirt, his work-hewn hands clutching a wide-brimmed straw hat. Rachel wore a modest black dress and lace-up boots, and beneath the white head covering indicating her married status, her light brown hair was pulled back in a tight bun. She was a pretty girl with a spattering of freckles on the bridge of her nose and the kindest brown eyes Derek had ever seen.

Several of Derek's patients hailed from the Amish village that bordered Eden Falls. As a physician, he appreciated the hardworking and serious nature of the Amish, and he offered his medical services to all the Amish folk of Paradise Ridge free of charge. Derek had never been one to play favorites, but he had to admit, he held a real soft spot for Rachel and Jacob, a newly married couple only a few years older than his sixteen-year-old sister.

His heart had sunk to the pit of his stomach during Rachel's examination. Informing a patient that he'd discovered a lump in her breast was pure agony, especially when the patient happened to be a sweet young woman only starting out in life. Rachel and Jacob had been shaken up by the news, but they'd put on brave faces as Derek wrote up the referral to an oncologist at Philly General.

Now, discreetly loitering by his receptionist's desk, Derek watched the exchange happening across the room, wondering why he couldn't shake the unsettling feeling churning in his gut.

Amelia had been unusually jumpy today. Scratch that—she was *always* jumpy, which was probably why he constantly found himself second-guessing his decision to hire her.

He couldn't deny her skill, though. The woman was damn good at her job, possessing a gentle bedside manner and the kind of swift efficiency he couldn't help but admire. She'd displayed courage and grace under pressure when she'd helped him treat Violet Chastain, despite having been thrust into the task right in the middle of her job interview. She'd impressed the hell out of him then, and she continued to impress him now.

But…something about the woman didn't sit right with him. He got the feeling there was a lot more to Amelia Phillips than met the eye, but he'd yet to figure out if she was secretive by nature or just keeping secrets.

"Derek?"

Amelia's soft voice jolted him from his thoughts. He looked up to find her standing directly in front of him. A glance at the door showed that the Danfords had taken their leave.

"Sorry. I spaced out." He cleared his throat. "What were you talking with Rachel and Jacob about?"

She flushed. "I offered to be at the hospital with them when Rachel goes in for the biopsy." She quickly hurried on. "I know that striking up a friendship with a patient might be construed as unprofessional, but I feel so badly for the girl. And she and Jacob are terrified of hospitals, so I thought seeing a familiar face when she gets the procedure done might be comforting."

Her words brought a pang of guilt to Derek's stomach. Damn, and a second ago he'd actually been rethinking his decision to hire this woman. That Amelia would go out of her way to ease Rachel Danford's anxiety told him far more about her than her tendency to get skittish. He'd never met a woman with a bigger heart, and as she fidgeted awkwardly, awaiting his response, Derek had to smile.

"That's a really nice thought," he said gruffly.

Her blush deepened, drawing his attention to those smooth, ivory cheeks of hers.

It was probably inappropriate as hell, checking out his nurse, but could anyone really blame him? Amelia Phillips was one fine-looking woman. Heartbreakingly beautiful, in fact. She had the kind of ethereal beauty that took your breath away—wide-set hazel eyes and shoulder-length blond hair that looked so soft to the touch his fingers tingled with the need to stroke it. She was average height, but next to his six-foot frame she seemed utterly petite, and she had a curvy, hourglass body that made his mouth go dry. He'd never understood why some men lusted over super-skinny women with their rib cages poking out. In Derek's opinion, there was nothing sexier than a soft, womanly form you could fill your palms with, and Amelia had that in spades.

He knew from her job application that she was forty-one, but she certainly didn't look it. She could easily pass for twenty-five, and he could only imagine the looks she got when she walked down the street. That smoking-hot body of hers probably stopped traffic.

That smoking-hot body belongs to your nurse, buddy.

Derek quickly snapped his brain out of the gutter. Yeah, he definitely needed to quit focusing on Amelia Phillips's centerfold assets and concentrate on other things—like the fact that she *worked* for him.

"Oh, and both Stu Robertson and Maggie Carpenter canceled their appointments," Amelia went on, oblivious to his wickedly improper thoughts, "so the rest of your afternoon is officially clear. Nancy left a note about it before she left for the day."

"Sawyer will be disappointed," Derek said wryly. "He was hoping to practice his doctoring today."

"I'm here!"

Speak of the devil.

Derek's mouth lifted in a smile as his little brother burst through the door and skidded across the small lobby area. The eleven-year-old's head shot in the direction of the waiting room off to the left. When he found it empty, his expression collapsed.

"Am I too late?" Sawyer demanded. "I had detention, but it only lasted fifteen minutes. I ran all the way over here." Which explained why his cheeks held a ruddy glow and his sandy-colored hair was sticking up in every direction.

Derek felt a rush of warmth when he glimpsed the disappointment in his brother's eyes. Sawyer had been making a habit of coming to the clinic after school, shadowing his big brother and soaking up medical knowledge like a sponge. The kid kept going back and forth about what he wanted to be when he grew up—a doctor like Derek or a cop like their brother Tate—but lately medicine had been winning out, and Derek had to admit that he enjoyed having Sawyer around.

"Sorry, Squirt, our last two patients canceled," he said, ruffling Sawyer's hair. "But you could always keep me company while I do some paperwork."

"Bo-ring." Mr. Unobservant that he was, Sawyer suddenly noticed Amelia standing there. "Amelia, hi!"

The kid launched himself at her, wrapping his gangly arms around her waist.

Derek didn't miss the way Amelia flinched when Sawyer hugged her or the way she didn't return the embrace.

Again, that flicker of wariness tugged on his gut. Amelia seemed completely ill at ease around his little brother. Around all children, in fact. She handled the younger patients the same way she did the older ones—with extreme warmth and professionalism—but Derek had noticed on numerous occasions that she didn't seem entirely comfortable with kids.

Sawyer, however, was more than comfortable with Amelia. For some reason, the kid had taken a real shining to the beautiful blonde. Adored her, actually.

Trying to ease her evident discomfort, Derek tugged on the collar of Sawyer's striped T-shirt and pinned the kid with a deadly stare. "What was that I heard about detention?"

Sawyer raised his hands in a defensive gesture. "Don't look at me. Danny Harris talked back to Ms. Bentley and we all got punished for it. Totally unfair if you ask me."

Derek's lips twitched. "I guess that was Ms. Bentley's way of sending the rest of you a message. A warning of what happens when you sass her."

"Doesn't make it any less unfair," Sawyer grumbled, before turning to Amelia in interest. "So what are you gonna do while Derek does his paperwork?"

She cast Derek a quizzical look. "Well, boss, what *am* I going to do?"

"You get to go home," he answered. When she looked ready to protest, he held up his hand. "You deserve some time off. Now that you're a permanent fixture in this practice, I plan on working you to the bone, so enjoy the break while it lasts."

She laughed softly. "I guess I can use the time to assemble some furniture. I ordered a bunch of things online after I moved into my place but I haven't gotten around to any of it yet."

"Bo-ring," Sawyer chimed again. He suddenly clapped a hand on his leg. "You should come to dinner tonight. We are making brownies for dessert."

Amelia started to edge away, her hip bumping the desk. "Oh. That's a nice offer, but I don't know if I can."

"You just said you don't have anything to do," Sawyer said in an accusatory tone. "So you can totally come."

Derek sighed. "Sawyer—"

"Please?" his brother pleaded. "I want you to see the ranch and my horse, and did I tell you we're making brownies?"

Amelia smiled indulgently. "Yes, I think you mentioned that."

"So...please?"

She shifted awkwardly. "I guess I could." She glanced at Derek. "If it's okay with your brother, that is."

"You're welcome to join us," he said gruffly.

After a beat, she nodded. "All right. What time?"

"Seven o'clock," Sawyer piped up.

"Okay. Well. I guess I'll be there." She took a few steps toward the corridor behind them. "I should change out of these scrubs."

As Amelia dashed off, Derek released a heavy breath and turned to his brother with a frown. "What did I tell you about putting people on the spot, Squirt?"

Sawyer had the decency to blush. "I know. I'm sorry. But I really want Amelia to come to dinner. You want her to come, too, right?"

"Sure," he said noncommittally.

The kid tilted his head. "So I did good, right? It could be like a date."

Derek faltered. "No, not like a date. Amelia and I work together, Squirt. That's all there is to it."

"Is it because of Aunt Tess?"

Now he froze. "What do you mean?"

"Piper says that you're still mourning Aunt Tess," Sawyer said frankly. "I told her that's silly because Aunt Tess died a long time ago."

Two years wasn't a long time, he wanted to point out, but he supposed that for an eleven-year-old, two years was an eternity.

He couldn't believe they were even having this conversation. Nobody in the family dared bring up Tess's name to him, and truth be told, he preferred it that way. Just thinking about his wife sent a hot rush of agony to his chest. It was funny, how he'd nagged his brother Gunnar to see a counselor in order to deal with his tragic experience in Afghanistan, yet if Derek were being honest with himself, he hadn't fully dealt with his own tragedy.

Tess's death still ate at him. It gnawed at his insides like a hungry scavenger, making it impossible to move on—yes, even two *long* years later.

"Because if it is about Aunt Tess," Sawyer went on, oblivious to Derek's silence, "I think that's dumb."

His throat clogged. "Why is that dumb?"

"Because Aunt Tess wasn't a very good wife."

Out of the mouths of babes.

"Why do you say that?" His voice was so hoarse it felt as if someone had shoved sand into his mouth.

"Because she made you sad," Sawyer said simply.

An arrow of pain pierced Derek's heart. He knew he shouldn't be surprised by his little brother's observation. He and Tess had been having trouble long before her death—and clearly, the rest of his family had noticed.

Swallowing a lump of regret, Derek clapped a hand on Sawyer's scrawny shoulder. "Let's stop all this serious talk. What do you say I forget about my pesky paperwork and take you out for some hot chocolate instead?"

The kid's eyes lit up. "Seriously?"

"Seriously. Go sit in the waiting room while I gather up my things, okay?"

"Cool beans."

Sawyer bounded off just as Amelia reemerged from the corridor. She'd changed out of her green scrubs and now wore a pair of snug blue jeans that hugged her shapely legs, a tight-fitting brown sweater that brought out the amber flecks in her hazel eyes and high-heeled black boots. With her silky blond hair tied back in a ponytail, she looked young and fresh-faced and utterly gorgeous.

"I'm heading out," she told him as she shrugged into her black wool coat, then put on a pair of brown leather gloves. "Should I bring anything?"

He wrinkled his brow.

"For dinner," she clarified. "Wine? Dessert?"

"Nope. Just bring yourself."

He realized at the last second how flirty that sounded, and the blush that rose on her cheeks confirmed it.

Derek gulped, wondering why he was so damn drawn to this woman. For the past two years he hadn't felt a single inkling to get involved with anyone. Actually, he'd vowed to steadfastly avoid relationships altogether.

Yet from the moment Amelia Phillips walked into his clinic, he hadn't been able to fight the spark of desire she evoked inside him.

"Okay. Well." Her delicate throat worked as she visibly swallowed. "I'll see you tonight."

Derek bid her goodbye, then watched as she gracefully strode toward the door and exited the clinic. Everything about that woman intrigued him, from her soft, melodic voice to the shadowy secrets lurking in her hazel eyes.

Maybe having her over for dinner tonight wasn't such a bad idea, after all. Amelia Phillips continued to remain a mystery, and his inquisitive nature didn't mesh well with riddles. It drove him absolutely crazy that he still couldn't get a real handle on his beautiful new nurse. That he had no idea why her face took on that haunted expression when she thought nobody was looking. He hadn't felt comfortable grilling her here, while they worked side by side, but perhaps she'd be more willing to open up outside the professional confines of the clinic.

Perhaps tonight he would finally get some answers from the elusive Amelia.

Chapter 2

Chloe had never been more nervous in her entire life as she drove through the double gates of the Colton ranch. The main house was visible in the distance, a large homestead that managed to combine the stately elegance of a manor with the rustic charm of a ranch spread. It wasn't the size or beauty of the home that made her anxious—she was no stranger to expensive accommodations—but the homey, inviting feel of it. The yellow glow seeping from the windows, the tire swing hanging from one of the trees in the front yard. It was the kind of place she'd always envisioned raising a family in, and the thought brought a sharp pain to her heart.

Her hands trembled on the steering wheel of the used Toyota hatchback she'd purchased last week. Why on Earth had she agreed to have dinner with the Coltons tonight? When Derek had invited her to his family's Thanksgiving dinner last week, she'd had no problem politely declining. So why had it been so hard to say no to *Sawyer's* request? Why had she allowed a tow-headed kid to break down her defenses?

The thought of Sawyer Colton deepened the ache in her chest. Lord, that kid was a real charmer, not to mention precocious, sweet and wise beyond his years. But every time he came around, which was often, she experienced a wave of longing so powerful that tears stung her eyes. She liked to imagine that her own boys would have grown up to be exactly like Sawyer.

Focus, Chloe.

Choking down a lump of sorrow, she continued up the driveway, but halfway to the main house another fit of anxiety rippled through her and her foot came down on the brakes. A minute. She just needed a minute to collect her composure.

Flipping down the sun visor, she studied her reflection, inspecting her left cheek. Makeup looked good. No hint of the four-inch scar beneath it.

Still, simply knowing the imperfection existed made her feel self-conscious as hell.

"You think you're so beautiful, don't you, Chloe? Pretty, pretty Chloe."

A tornado of pain, fury and bitterness spiraled through her as Felix's cruel voice echoed in her head.

"All those men flirting with my beautiful wife. You liked it, didn't you, pretty Chloe? You like feeling beautiful?"

Hot tears pricked her eyelids. She tried desperately to block the memories, but they barreled into her mind like a freight train. Felix had been so enraged that night, yet again blaming her for something beyond her control.

"Let's see if men still find you attractive now, shall we?"

A phantom burst of agony exploded in her face, mimicking everything she'd felt when the blade of that scalpel sliced into her cheek.

Sucking in a ragged breath, Chloe forcibly shoved the horrific memory from her mind. She couldn't fall apart right now. Not in her boss's driveway, for Pete's sake.

Exhaling slowly, she moved the gearshift to Drive and steered toward the main house. After she'd parked the car, she grabbed her purse and the apple pie she'd picked up at the bakery in town, then climbed the large porch and rang the bell.

Footsteps thudded. A second later the front door swung open and an attractive redhead appeared before her. Chloe instantly recognized Emma Colton, Derek's younger sister and a field agent with the FBI. They'd met when Emma had interviewed Violet Chastain at the clinic after the actress's attack.

"Amelia," Emma said, sounding genuinely happy to see her. "We're thrilled to have you." She opened the door wider. "Come in."

Chloe stepped into the spacious front hall and shrugged out of her coat. Emma took it from her, hanging it in the closet by the door.

"I brought dessert," Chloe said, holding out the pie dish. "Sawyer mentioned something about brownies, but I figured I'd bring something, anyway."

"Thanks. That was really sweet of you," Emma answered with a smile.

Chloe glanced around, admiring the wood-paneled walls and pretty oil-painted landscapes hanging in the space. "You have a lovely home."

Emma grinned. "Technically you should be saying that to Derek. He owns the ranch now."

"Really? I had no idea."

"He doesn't advertise it. My brother is a doctor first and a rancher second, but Mom and Dad left him the homestead in their will because Derek's always been the most responsible Colton in the bunch." Emma anticipated Chloe's question before she could voice it. "Don't worry, there's no hidden resentment or anything—I think Gunnar and Tate were as relieved as I was that we didn't have to take on the responsibility of this place."

Emma led her into the great room, which featured endless ceilings, comfortable brown leather couches and a stone fireplace. Derek's teenage sister, Piper, sat on one of the sofas, holding a blond-haired toddler in her arms. On the floor, Derek's brother Tate was sprawled on the thick rug next to a second toddler. Although the two little boys were identical, they clearly had their own distinct personalities—the one on the couch was content to sit calmly in Piper's arms, while the terror on the floor busied himself with a set of colorful blocks, shrieking in delight each time Tate leaned over to tickle him.

"Violet Chastain's twins," Emma said, noticing Chloe staring. "We're babysitting Mason and Hudson tonight so Violet and Gunnar can have some alone time at the cabin."

Chloe tore her gaze from the adorable little boys, ignoring the rush of longing that filled her belly. She focused on Tate, who greeted her with a warm smile. "Hey, Amelia. Where's Mr. Perfect?"

She shot him a blank look.

"Derek," Tate clarified with a crooked grin. "You know, the perfect doctor, perfect brother, perfect everything."

The amusement dancing in Tate's aqua eyes told her it was all in good fun, but it didn't surprise her that Derek's siblings called him Mr. Perfect. The man epitomized perfection— handsome, talented, kind, sexy. Derek Colton was the real deal, no doubt about it.

"He's not here?" she said, frowning.

"Derek doesn't live in the big house," Piper spoke up as she intercepted the toddler's chubby hand before he could grab a hunk of her wispy blond hair. "His house is next door." The teenager glanced at Tate. "He texted me just now saying he's on his way."

"Have a seat," Emma said to Chloe. "Can I grab you a drink? Wine, beer, iced tea?"

"An iced tea would be great."

Chloe felt a tad awkward as she settled on the couch opposite Piper and folded her hands in her lap. This was her first official social visit since she'd moved to Eden Falls, and though she'd met all of Derek's siblings before, being surrounded by so many people at once was daunting. As an only child, she'd always wished for a brother or sister, someone to laugh with and spill her secrets to, someone other than herself who she could rely on.

Her discomfort grew the longer she sat there, watching the

scene before her. Tate teasing Piper, the happy squeals of Violet's twins and Emma's throaty laughter as she returned to the room with Sawyer hot on her heels.

Sawyer grinned when he spotted Chloe, making a beeline for her. "You came," he said happily. He fixed a stern look in his sister's direction, then glanced back at Chloe. "I hope Piper wasn't annoying you."

Chloe stifled a laugh. "Don't worry—Piper has been a perfect lady."

The boy snorted. "Right. The perfect *giant* lady, maybe. Piper is freakishly tall."

"Hello? I'm sitting right here, twerp," Piper said, waving her hand in the air. "At least have the decency to insult me behind my back."

"But it's more fun to do it to your face."

Chloe and Tate exchanged an amused look as the duo continued to bicker. Despite the insults being traded back and forth, it was clear that Piper and Sawyer adored each other.

The Coltons were an unusual bunch, Chloe thought as she listened to the group chatter amongst themselves. Different ages, sizes, races, hair color, eye color. Charlotte and Donovan Colton had run a nonprofit organization for inner-city children, and Derek had laughingly told her that they liked to bring their work home with them—case in point, the six children they'd adopted.

As she sipped the iced tea Emma brought her, the photographs displayed on the fireplace mantel caught her attention. Setting the drinking glass on the pine coffee table, Chloe stood and headed for the hearth, smiling as she focused on a photo featuring a happy, distinguished-looking couple.

"That's my mom and dad," Sawyer said, coming up beside her. "I didn't know them all that well. I was just a baby when they died." His somber expression brightened as he pointed to the framed photo next to the first one. "And that's me and Piper."

Chloe grinned. "Yeah, I can see that."

Sawyer then proceeded to point out each and every person in each and every picture, even the ones featuring only himself. Eventually, Chloe quit paying attention, until her gaze snagged on a photo of Derek with a pretty, raven-haired woman. The woman's features hinted at both American and Asian descent, and she was utterly petite, the top of her head barely coming up to Derek's shoulders. Both were beaming at the camera, but Chloe noticed that the smile didn't quite reach the woman's eyes. There was something so very sad about the woman in the picture.

"That's Aunt Tess," Sawyer said in a low voice, leaning closer to Chloe as if he didn't want anyone to overhear.

"Aunt Tess?" she whispered.

"Derek's wife. She died."

Shock blasted through her, but Chloe did her best to hide her reaction. Derek didn't wear a wedding ring—she'd definitely looked—but in the month she'd been working for him, he hadn't once mentioned a deceased wife. Judging by Sawyer's hushed tone, she got the feeling "Aunt Tess" wasn't a common topic of conversation in the Colton household.

"Finally," Tate said dryly.

Chloe turned around in time to see Derek stride into the room. Her heart did an involuntary somersault and she berated herself for the silly response.

Still, it was so hard not to drool over the man. Without the white coat and scrub bottoms he wore at the clinic, he looked far more approachable. Much more…well, sexy. His khakis were loose but couldn't hide the long, muscular legs beneath them, and his black sweater molded to his broad, rippled chest. Lord, the man definitely worked out—no way had he acquired that rock-hard physique by handling a stethoscope and taking someone's blood pressure.

She tore her eyes off his chest, moved them to his face

and offered a timid smile. "Hey, Doct—Derek," she quickly amended.

His easy smile warmed her insides. "Hey, Amelia. Glad you could make it."

"I appreciate the invitation."

Their eyes locked from across the room, and Chloe could have sworn she heard the air crackle. Or maybe it was the sound of her heart hammering against her breasts. She couldn't remember the last time she'd been so drawn to a man. Even her husband hadn't intrigued her the way Derek Colton did.

She gulped.

You don't have a husband. You're Amelia Phillips.

"Come on, little dudes, go to Julia."

Piper's voice jolted Chloe from her thoughts. A dark-haired woman—Julia, Chloe assumed—scooped up the toddlers, propped one on each of her hips and headed for the door.

"That's our nanny," Sawyer explained, tugging on Chloe's hand.

"She's going to watch the little terrors while we eat," Derek added. "Violet's nanny also has a much-deserved night off." He shook his head in amazement. "I don't know how Violet does it. Those two never seem to run out of energy."

"I don't know how *Gunnar* will do it," Tate corrected with a laugh.

"Dinner's ready, guys!" Emma called, poking her head into the living room.

As the group trudged toward the kitchen, Chloe felt a hand on her arm. She jumped in surprise, then relaxed when she realized it was Derek.

"Always so jumpy," he murmured.

"You startled me."

"You're easily startled, aren't you, Amelia?"

The contemplative note in his deep voice heightened her unease. She met his gaze and saw that his brown eyes were studying her, searching, probing, as if he were trying to bore right into her head.

She managed a faint smile. "I need to stop being so skittish, huh? I think it's the move—new town, new job, new friends. It always takes me a while to adjust to new situations."

After a beat, he nodded and gently squeezed her arm. "It'll take some time, but I have a feeling you'll fit right in. Come on, let's have some dinner."

Family dinners topped Derek's list of favorite events, probably because they'd been so important to the couple who'd adopted him when he was three years old.

Charlotte and Donovan Colton had been the strongest, most loving people he'd ever met. They'd taken not just one child into their home, but six, and Derek and his siblings had grown up surrounded by so much love that his heart now boasted a big hole thanks to the loss of his parents.

Derek had insisted on keeping the tradition of weekly family dinners that had meant so much to his parents. Surrounded by his brothers and sisters, he felt a sense of peace that had been lacking in his life the past couple of years. Ever since Tess's accident, he'd been having a tough time finding his footing again.

Professionally, he was as confident and composed as ever, but when he walked into his empty house at night, that cool and collected air he'd mastered dissolved, leaving him with a deep ache in his gut and a rush of loneliness. Despite everything they'd gone through, everything she'd put him through, he missed Tess. Or maybe he missed the woman she'd once been, the sweet girl he'd fallen in love with during college. Either way, he couldn't deny the emptiness he felt, the sorrow that consumed him whenever he found himself alone with his thoughts.

"So your family lives in Missouri, then?" Emma asked.

Derek raised his head, realizing his mind had wandered.

Emma's question had been directed at Amelia, whose expression creased with pain.

"My mother passed away about fifteen years ago," Amelia admitted. "But yes, my father's in Missouri."

Derek sensed there was more to the story, but the flicker of sorrow in Amelia's big hazel eyes told him not to go there. His little brother, however, had yet to perfect the art of tact.

"Your dad lives alone?" Sawyer asked between mouthfuls of his meat loaf. "He didn't get married again after your mom died?"

"Sawyer," Tate chided. "Enough with the Twenty Questions."

"It's okay," Amelia said softly. "I don't mind." Her fork toyed with the mashed potatoes on her plate, but she seemed to have lost her appetite. "My father didn't remarry. He's actually living in an assisted care facility just outside of St. Louis."

Derek's heart clenched as he met her eyes.

"Early-onset Alzheimer's," she revealed, as if she'd heard his silent question.

Derek nodded. "When was he diagnosed?"

"When he was fifty-five. That was ten years ago."

"I'm sorry, Amelia," Emma spoke up. "That must be so difficult, seeing someone you love go through something like that."

Amelia cast her eyes downward. "It's been very difficult."

A lull fell over the table, until Tate cleared his throat and changed the subject. As Tate and Emma began discussing the investigation into the missing Amish girls, Derek discreetly studied Amelia from across the table. The revelation about her father was the first nugget of information he'd gleaned from her since he'd hired her three weeks ago, but it still wasn't enough.

Amelia Phillips fascinated him like no other woman ever had. On the surface she seemed so fragile, but after working with her, he knew she had a core of steel. She was incredible with patients, met any challenge head-on and, when she let her guard down, displayed a witty sense of humor that never failed to make him smile.

But what else did he really know about her? She'd gone to college in California and worked there as a nurse for eight years, then moved back to Missouri and spent the next ten years doing God knows what before resuming her nursing career. Why such a long hiatus? Why had she moved to Pennsylvania? And why on Earth was she still single? Considering her youthful beauty and sweet demeanor, he couldn't fathom that.

By the time dessert was served, Derek wasn't any closer to getting the answers to those questions. And because he doubted she'd divulge any information while surrounded by his siblings, when Sawyer and Piper began to clear the table, he turned to Amelia and said, "How about a tour of the ranch?"

There it was again—that startled look in her eyes. "Oh. Sure," she agreed awkwardly.

"Can I come?" Sawyer asked as he juggled the dishes in his hands.

"No, you can help your sisters clean up," Tate answered for Derek.

When he met his brother's eyes and saw the knowing gleam in them, Derek realized Tate knew he'd been hoping to get Amelia alone.

Battling a pang of discomfort, Derek averted his eyes and scraped back his chair. "You can come along next time," he told Sawyer when he noticed the disappointment on the boy's face.

Sawyer frowned but didn't protest, which Derek was incredibly grateful for at the moment.

As he led Amelia out of the kitchen, he told himself that this inexplicable urge to get to know her was simply a result of his innate curiosity. Even as a kid he'd hungered for knowledge, needing to make sense of the world and the people around him. He'd never known his birth parents, and the foster families he'd lived with for the first three years of his life were nothing but a shadowy blur to him. As a result, he'd developed a need to make connections, to truly *know* the people in his life.

"We'll take my car," he said after he and Amelia put on their coats in the front hall.

She raised one dark-blond brow. "This isn't a walking tour?"

"Trust me, you'll thank me later. The ranch is too big to wander around on foot."

Ten minutes later, as they drove through the sprawling compound, Amelia turned to him with a laugh. "Wow. You're right. This place is huge."

As he pointed out the various outbuildings and landmarks, Derek discovered that he enjoyed seeing the Double C through Amelia's eyes. He suddenly realized he'd stopped paying attention to the scenery of the ranch he'd lived on all his life. His practice kept him so busy that he rarely ventured out of his comfortable brick home, which neighbored the big house, and he had no need to oversee the ranching operation, since their foreman, Hank, was more than capable of handling the day-to-day activities.

But as Amelia oohed and ahhed at her surroundings, Derek experienced a burst of pride. The Double C truly was spectacular, the landscape marked by rolling wooded hills, large paddocks and rustic outbuildings. Eden Falls had yet to see a heavy snow, but the layer of silver frost dusting the land hinted that winter would finally be making an appearance soon.

Pointing to the left, he turned to Amelia and said, "There's a little stream about half a mile that way. It's probably too cold to walk along the bank right now, but I'll take you out there in the spring. It's a really beautiful little spot."

"That sounds nice," she said in a noncommittal tone.

A fresh wave of unease swelled in his gut, prompting him to pull to the side of the dirt trail and put the car in Park. As determination hardened his jaw, he shifted in the driver's seat and faced Amelia.

"Who are you?" he asked.

Shock flooded her eyes. "Wh-what?"

"Who are you, Amelia? We've been working together for three weeks, yet I still don't know a thing about you. Why did you move to Eden Falls? What do you do for fun? Tell me something that nobody else knows about you."

Her shoulders, which had been stiff a second ago, relaxed slightly. With a tiny shrug, she offered him a gentle smile. "There's not much to know. If I'm being honest, I'm not a very interesting person."

"I don't believe that." Not one bit. Because whatever she claimed, she *did* interest him. Far too much for his liking, in fact.

Realizing he wouldn't drop the subject, Amelia released a sigh. "Well, you know why I moved to Eden Falls—for this job."

"You ran out of gas, stopped in town for lunch and saw my ad in the paper," he filled in, repeating the story she'd told him during her job interview.

"Yep." She shrugged again. "Like I said, I was heading for Philly, hoping to find work at one of the hospitals there, but the moment I stepped into Eden Falls, I knew this was where I belonged. This town is…it's…*home.* Know what I mean?"

"Yeah, actually I do," he admitted.

"As for what I do for fun? Not much," she said wryly. She pursed those lush lips, tilting her head in thought. "I used to volunteer a lot, mostly with hospital and children's charities."

"And what else?" he prompted. "What else do you like to do, Amelia?"

She hesitated and frustration bubbled in his stomach. Drawing details out of this woman was even harder than getting that terror Billy Hanson to sit still for his annual vaccinations.

"I love to bake," she finally confessed. "I'm a whiz at crossword puzzles. I'm scared of bugs. I like to draw, but I'm not very good at it. I hate television—I only watch the news or DVDs. I'm not very outdoorsy, but I do like to ski."

Well, that was a start.

Sensing that she was warming up to this sharing thing, Derek decided to do some more digging. "Why did you quit nursing after you left California? You're a natural at it."

He noticed the pulse point in her throat jump, as if he'd broached a subject she wasn't entirely comfortable with. "I had no choice," she said after a beat. "My father was diagnosed with Alzheimer's and someone had to take care of him. My mother was gone and I don't have any siblings, so my dad had nobody else."

"So you gave up your career to take care of your father?" When she nodded, he whistled softly. "You must be very close to him, then."

She slowly shook her head. "We weren't close, at least not while I was growing up. My mother was…let's just say controlling. And appearances were the only thing that mattered to her. She expected me to marry a wealthy man and spend my time sitting on committees and hosting dinner parties. When I told her I wanted to be a nurse, she pretty much disowned me. We weren't even speaking when she died."

Amelia swallowed. "I rarely saw my dad during those years. My mother made it clear that I wasn't welcome, at least not until I stopped being so stubborn and lived the kind of life she wanted me to."

Derek frowned. "And your father just sat by and let all this happen?"

"He let her call the shots," she said sadly. "He knew I wanted more from my life, but he took my mother's lead." She gulped again. "I'd hoped Dad and I would get closer after she died, and we did—for a brief time. But the closeness only lasted a year or so. Then he was diagnosed, and now…" She let out a shaky breath. "Now he doesn't even know who I am."

As his heart constricted, Derek reached across the armrest and took her hand. She jerked in surprise, her gaze flying to his, but she didn't pull her hand away.

Her skin was hot to the touch and so very smooth. Derek's pulse quickened, a rush of desire flooding his body as Amelia gently rubbed her thumb over the center of his palm. Christ. He couldn't remember the last time he'd held a woman's hand. Consoling overwrought patients didn't count; he frequently offered comfort to the folks he treated. But this was different. This was…terrifying.

Struggling to steady the erratic thudding of his heart, he slowly brought his hand back to the steering wheel, avoiding Amelia's eyes. "Shall we continue the tour?" he asked thickly.

"Actually, um, maybe we should head back." From the corner of his eye, he saw her edging closer to the door, as if trying to put distance between them. "I really do need to get started fixing up my apartment."

He ignored the disappointment that clenched his insides, knowing it was for the best if she left now. This strange attraction to Amelia Phillips unsettled him. He wasn't looking to get involved with anyone—not now and not in the future. Besides, Amelia was his nurse. He signed her paychecks, for chrissake.

"Yeah, that's probably a good idea," he said as he executed a U-turn and steered the car back in the direction of the main house. "Now that you're sticking around in Eden Falls, you'll need a cozy place to go home to."

By the time they reached the ranch house, Amelia looked as relieved as Derek felt. She practically launched herself out of the passenger seat, then shot him a nervous smile. "I had a nice time, Derek. Please thank your family for a lovely dinner."

"Will do," he said gruffly. "Have a good night, Amelia. Drive safe."

"Night, Derek."

As he watched her hurry toward her car, he reached up to rub the five-o'clock shadow dotting his jaw and wondered why the hell this woman affected him so damn much.

* * *

Chloe's heart raced as she drove away from the Double C. Rolling farmland and rustic houses flashed by the car window, but she couldn't pay attention to the scenery, not when Derek's baritone voice continued to run through her mind.

Who are you?

In that moment, she'd feared he'd figured out her secret—that she wasn't Amelia Phillips, but Chloe Moreno, the woman who'd faked a suicide and fled to the other end of the country to escape her husband.

Funny enough, when she'd realized that Derek wasn't interrogating her, but just trying to get to know her better, her panic only intensified. The more time she spent with Derek Colton, the more she liked him, but she knew she couldn't let herself open up to him, no matter how badly she wanted to. Felix might believe she was dead, but it would take a long time for Chloe to feel safe again.

The clip-clop of horse hooves caught her attention and she slowed the car, stopping to let a horse and buggy cross. The bearded Amish man at the reins wore a dark-colored suit and a black hat with a wide brim. He nodded in thanks as their eyes met through the windshield, and Chloe managed a weak smile. Sometimes she envied the Amish citizens residing in the area. Their lives were so simple, revolving around hard work, humility and family. She'd give her right arm for that simplicity, for just one day without this deep ache in her bones.

Simple doesn't mean safe.

The ominous reminder had her spirits sinking even lower. God, nothing and nobody were immune to danger and heartache. The missing Paradise Ridge girls were proof of that.

As the buggy disappeared down the darkness-bathed road, Chloe continued straight, driving into the heart of town. The downtown shops had closed for the night, but the glow of the lampposts lining the streets illuminated the windows and drew her gaze to the holiday decorations gracing the storefronts.

This would be her first Christmas in twelve years without Felix. The realization made her think back to the very start of their marriage, when she'd been young and foolish and completely in love with the older, distinguished doctor.

All her life she'd been nagged by her high-society mother to marry a successful man. She was taught to hold her tongue and look pretty, to aspire for nothing more than the security a husband could offer. Ironically, she'd thought she was defying her mother when she'd married Felix. She'd met him while working in the trauma unit at the hospital in L.A.; back then he'd been an up-and-coming plastic surgeon, immediately sucking her in with his dark good-looks and undeniable charm. He'd actually valued her opinion, encouraging her to speak her mind, challenging her with thought-provoking discussions, treating her like a worthy partner rather than the daughter of Martin and Lynn Hathaway, a pair of wealthy Midwest transplants to Beverly Hills.

She should've recognized Felix's controlling nature when he convinced her to quit nursing and demanded she stay at home, but he'd seemed so eager to start a family with her. And she'd wanted the same thing—to be a mother to Felix's children. She wanted it so badly she'd agreed to concentrate on their marriage and soon-to-be family rather than her career.

But now she was on the other side of the country, choking down the bitter taste in her mouth and parking her Toyota in the tiny parking lot at the rear of her two-story apartment building. She had to stop thinking about Felix and focus on the fresh start she'd been presented with.

Fishing her keys out of her purse, she locked the car and headed for the back entrance of the building. Her apartment was on the second floor, but the building didn't have an elevator so she had to climb the rickety wooden stairs, which squeaked beneath her boots.

When she reached her apartment, the door swung open before she could even turn the key.

She winced. The latch on the door had been loose since she'd moved in, but she hadn't gotten around to fixing it yet. Besides, after three weeks in Eden Falls, she'd discovered that hardly anyone locked their doors around here. The crime rate in town was zero—or at least it had been until those Amish girls had begun disappearing.

Entering her apartment, Chloe made a mental note to get the doorknob fixed tomorrow. After the attempted kidnapping of Violet Chastain, she really needed to take better precautions.

Right, because a scarred, middle-aged woman is a mighty draw for a sex ring.

Fine, so the sick perverts snatching up those innocent girls probably wouldn't take a second look at Chloe Moreno aka Amelia Phillips. But that didn't mean she shouldn't be more careful.

After she removed her outerwear and tossed her purse on the plaid-upholstered couch she'd purchased from the sole furniture store in town, she ducked into her small kitchen and brewed herself a cup of tea. She still had that bookshelf to assemble, but at the moment she wanted nothing more than to sit on the sofa, watch the ten o'clock news and clear her head.

Heading back to the living room, she set her tea on the square glass coffee table, then settled on the couch. She drew a flannel blanket around her legs and flicked the remote control.

The second the screen came to life, sound blared from the television speakers.

"I, Chloe, take you, Felix, to be my lawfully wedded husband."

Horror slammed into Chloe's chest with the force of a sledgehammer.

Her eyes nearly bugged out of their sockets as she stared at her younger self on the television screen. Clad in an elaborate lace gown with a scoop neckline and full skirt, twenty-nine-year-old Chloe gazed up at her dark-haired husband-to-be with pure adoration. A white-robed priest stood before the happy couple with a leather prayer book in his hands. In the background, the soft strains of violins could be heard.

Her wedding. Dear God, this was her wedding video.

The video she'd left behind when she fled Malibu.

"I, Felix Moreno, take you, Chloe, to be my…"

Chloe leaped off the couch as if she'd discovered a cockroach in her lap. But no, this was worse than a cockroach. Far more terrifying than her irrational fear of insects.

He was here.

Felix was here.

Panic torpedoed through her. Acid burned her throat, making it impossible to breathe. She sucked in shallow breaths, her body trembling so violently she keeled over, sagging against the arm of the couch for balance. Her wild gaze landed on the DVD player, which was whirring away, the seconds ticking off on the display.

She stood there frozen for several long seconds, then she burst into action, grabbing the first object she saw—a heavy glass paperweight sitting on the coffee table.

Swallowing her fear, Chloe crept toward the narrow hallway leading to her bedroom. As she approached the closed door, her heart thudded against her ribs and her lungs ached, prompting her to take a deep breath.

Call the cops, a little voice ordered.

She faltered in front of the bedroom. If her husband truly was behind that door, she had no chance of fighting him off. Felix was bigger than her, and his anger had always given him an inhuman amount of strength.

She had to call the police, then run out of the apartment and wait until the cops showed up to apprehend Felix.

But what if Felix *wasn't* here? What if she called for help and then had to explain to the responding officer why a simple DVD posed such a monumental threat to her? She'd have to confess to the police who she really was, and the news would then find its way to Felix. She'd pretty much be *announcing* to her husband that she was still alive.

When her palms started tingling and black dots danced in front of her eyes, she realized she'd forgotten to breathe again. Sucking oxygen into her lungs, she straightened her shoulders and tightened her grip on the paperweight. She couldn't risk calling the cops. Technically, no crime had even been committed—her door had been unlatched and nothing had been stolen as far as she knew.

Gathering her courage, she reached for the doorknob and turned it ever so slowly. Then she braced herself, half expecting Felix to burst out and grab her.

But nothing happened.

She pushed the door open, lifted the arm holding the paperweight and burst into the bedroom.

Empty.

The room was empty. And the closet door was wide-open, revealing more empty space because she still hadn't gotten around to hanging any of her clothes.

Relief skyrocketed through her. Taking another breath, she ducked out of the room and repeated the same process with the little bathroom across the hall.

Empty.

Chloe's shoulders relaxed, but tension continued to seize her muscles. Soft voices wafted through the apartment, followed by a burst of applause as the guests who'd attended her wedding cheered for the happy couple.

Feeling as if she'd just had the wind knocked out of her, Chloe trudged back to the living room and sank onto the couch. Her gaze fixed on the screen, on the broad smile gracing young Chloe's eyes as she walked down the aisle arm-in-arm with her new husband.

Only two copies of that wedding video existed. One sat on the shelf of her father's room at the nursing home in St. Louis, and she doubted Martin Hathaway even knew it was there and doubted even more that he'd suddenly regained his mental capacity, tracked her down to Eden Falls and left the video in her DVD player.

The other copy? Sitting in the entertainment system in the grand living room of her and Felix's beachfront mansion.

"He found me," she whispered, the agony-laced words echoing in the suddenly cold air of her apartment.

Chapter 3

"Amelia, I still need that file." A pause. "Amelia?" Another pause. *"Amelia."*

Chloe's hand snapped up at the sharp command. She turned to see Derek in the doorway of the filing room, his brown eyes flickering with annoyance. "What?" she asked absently.

"Stu Robertson's file," Derek repeated, sounding aggravated. "He'll be here any minute. He rescheduled his appointment, remember?"

"Oh, right, right. Sorry."

She darted toward the cabinet that housed the N-R files and flipped through the tabs until she found Stu Robertson's name. Her cheeks scorched with the heat of embarrassment as she handed Derek the folder.

Rather than leave the room, Derek tucked the file under one arm and eyed her warily. "Are you all right? You've been acting strange all morning."

No, I'm not all right! My psychotic husband left our wedding video in my apartment last night and I'm freaking out!

She bit back the words, deciding she didn't particularly feel like getting fired today. But she also didn't blame Derek for looking irritated. She'd been distracted from the moment she opened her eyes this morning. Well, that was not entirely true, considering she'd never gone to sleep in the first place. She'd spent the night tossing and turning in bed, clutching the paperweight and trying to convince her panic-ridden brain that if Felix planned on murdering her, he would've done it when she walked through the door hours before.

But no amount of convincing could make her believe that anyone other than Felix had left that horrific surprise for her.

Her husband knew she was alive. There was no other explanation for what happened last night, and although she didn't know why Felix hadn't just confronted her outright, the sick souvenir didn't really surprise her. Toying with people was Felix's favorite pastime. The man was a psychopath hiding behind a white coat and a prestigious reputation, and she knew better than anyone just how much he liked playing games.

"Amelia?"

Damn it. She'd spaced out. Again.

"I'm so sorry, Derek," she blurted, a streak of guilt soaring through her. "I've been a real pain in the ass today, haven't I?"

"I wouldn't put it quite that way, but…yeah." He offered a sheepish grin. "What's going on?"

"I didn't sleep well last night," she admitted. "I didn't sleep at all, actually."

He frowned, switching into doctor mode. "Are you prone to insomnia?"

"Not usually. It was just a fluke, I guess." She smiled. "Maybe it was the excitement of being offered a permanent position here."

He smiled back, and for the first time all morning she relaxed. Derek Colton's bone-melting smiles always had that effect on her. "I don't see how working for a small-town doctor could be very exciting, but thanks for the ego boost."

"Dr. Colton?" came Nancy's voice. "Stu Robertson is here."

Derek glanced over his shoulder at his receptionist. "Put him in exam room two, Nancy."

Chloe frowned. "Hey, that's my job, remember?"

"No," he corrected. "Right now, your job is to grab a cup

of coffee and unwind for an hour or so. Maybe the caffeine will wake you up."

Guilt prickled her skin. Wonderful. Her first day as a permanent fixture in the clinic, and she was being ordered to wake up.

Derek must have glimpsed the objection in her eyes because he chuckled. "I can handle Stu. He's only here to get a prescription for his arthritis medication. Go, Amelia. Drink some coffee, breathe some fresh air and come back when you're ready."

He strolled off before she could argue.

Chloe stared after him in dismay, feeling even guiltier when she heard Derek greet Stu Robertson in that deep, congenial voice of his. The clinic's appointment calendar was booked solid today, and instead of doing her job, she'd been so distracted that Derek had sent her away.

But she knew he'd made a good call. She'd be of no use to Derek or their patients if her brain wasn't firing on all cylinders.

Ducking into the small office where she stored her things, Chloe grabbed her coat and purse, then exited the clinic through the back door. Derek was right—the second she breathed in the crisp December air, she felt more alert. In a brisk pace, she walked to the café at the end of the block and ordered a large coffee, then sat on one of the tall-backed stools in front of the window that overlooked the quaint street.

Clasping her hands over the cardboard sleeve of her coffee cup, Chloe attempted to formulate a plan. She'd already replaced her loose door handle this morning; she'd been out the door at eight o'clock and waiting outside the hardware store when the owner opened up shop for the day. She hadn't been scheduled to work until nine, so she'd hurried home and installed the new handle, along with two shiny new dead bolts and a chain lock.

With that out of the way, she now had to—

Have to what? an incredulous voice demanded. *Now you leave town, Chloe!*

Her coffee cup froze before reaching her lips. Hands trembling, she set the foam cup on the counter and stared miserably out at the street.

Of course she had to leave town. What the hell other solution *was* there?

Felix clearly knew where she was—the little gift he'd left her last night proved it. And although Felix might be toying with her now, he wouldn't play the game forever. Eventually he would confront her.

He'll kill you.

Or worse, she thought with growing terror. She'd never imagined there *could* be anything worse than death, but Felix Moreno had shown her otherwise. She lifted her hand to her cheek, but even the scar was small potatoes compared to what Felix was capable of doing.

She couldn't risk staying in Eden Falls. If she stayed, she wouldn't just be placing her own life in jeopardy, but the lives of those around her.

Derek.

Her heart lurched at the thought. Felix wouldn't hesitate to hurt Derek, especially if he knew she'd gone to the Coltons' ranch for dinner yesterday evening. Her husband's jealous streak was vicious, and she already knew he didn't toss out empty threats.

"Something wrong with the coffee?"

Chloe shifted her head to see the barista behind the counter eyeing her warily. "No, it's fine."

"Oh. Because you've been sitting there for ten minutes and still haven't taken a single sip."

Ten minutes?

She hadn't realized she'd zoned out for that long. Sure enough, when she lifted her cup to her lips, the coffee she swallowed had grown lukewarm. But the caffeine managed to do its thing, kick-starting her brain and making her see that her best option—her only option—was to leave Eden Falls as soon as possible.

With a heavy heart, she slid off the stool and left the café, tossing her half-full cup into the trash can on the sidewalk. Her gaze landed on the quaint brick building at the end of the block, the clinic where she'd finally found a sense of purpose and belonging. The thought of giving up her job was pure torture.

So was the notion of never seeing Derek again.

She hadn't realized how much she'd come to like and respect him these past three weeks. How much she looked forward to seeing that gorgeous face of his every day, watching those capable hands tending to the patients who adored him.

Swallowing a lump of sorrow, Chloe returned to the clinic just as Stu Robertson was leaving. She smiled at the elderly man, then turned to Derek, who was bent over the reception desk murmuring something to Nancy. His white coat stretched over his broad back and shoulders, and she caught a glimpse of his handsome profile, those firm lips, that strong jaw, his proud forehead.

She fought a jolt of desire and a twinge of regret, wishing things could be different. That she could be the kind of woman that a man like Derek could fall in love with.

As if sensing her eyes on him, Derek turned, a half-smile lifting his lips. "Feeling better?" he asked.

At least stay for the rest of the day. You can't leave him in the lurch.

Chloe ignored the inner plea, knowing that if she was going to quit, leaving Derek in the lurch was *exactly* the way to do it. If she left in the most unprofessional, distasteful manner, then the chances of him tracking her down and begging her to stay would be nonexistent.

So rather than smiling back, she slowly shook her head in response to Derek's question.

His expression instantly sobered. "What's going on?"

She crossed the room on shaky legs, cast Nancy a discreet look, then met Derek's brown eyes. "Can we talk in your office for a moment?"

Amelia had quit.

She'd *quit*.

Derek still couldn't wrap his head around it.

After his nurse had pretty much sprinted out the door as if a psycho killer was chasing her, he'd desperately wanted to run after her, but he couldn't just walk away when he had a waiting room full of patients expecting to see him. For the first time in his life, he found himself cursing his success. A booming practice was every doctor's dream, but today, the endless string of appointments had become Derek's worst nightmare. All he wanted to do was find Amelia and try to make sense of what had happened. Instead, he'd forced himself to go about his day—seeing patients and updating charts—all the while fighting the urge to kick something.

Only yesterday she'd been thrilled to accept a permanent position. What the hell had changed?

I made a mistake.

Small-town life isn't for me, after all.

Her feeble excuses continued to flash through his head, burning a hole in his gut, which roiled with anger and frustration.

"Will you excuse me for a second?" Derek said, cutting Rita Vernon off midsentence.

The elderly patient wrinkled her nose. "Is something wrong?" She paled. "Do my symptoms sound serious?"

"No, no," he said quickly.

"High cholesterol? Anemia? Oh, God—please don't say cancer!"

Derek inwardly cursed Amelia for leaving him in the lurch like this. Mrs. Vernon was a bona fide hypochondriac who showed up at the clinic nearly every other day, but Amelia had

had a soothing effect on the woman the last time she'd come in, which had made Derek's job a helluva lot easier. Now he was on his own, and as he fielded Mrs. Vernon's panicked questions, his frustration levels skyrocketed.

"Mrs. Vernon, I'm fairly certain that you are of absolute perfect health. I just need to excuse myself so I can grab your file, okay?"

Because he'd forgotten to bring it into the exam room with him. Because that was *Amelia's* damn job.

Mrs. Vernon relaxed. "Oh. All right."

As Derek slid out the door and headed for the file room, he pulled his cell phone from the breast pocket of his coat and dialed his brother's number.

Tate picked up on the second ring. "Hey, Doc, what's up?"

"I need a favor."

"Hit me."

Balancing the phone on his shoulder, Derek yanked open the file cabinet. "Amelia just quit," he muttered. "Can you—"

"She quit?" Tate interrupted. "Why the hell did she do that?"

"Apparently St. Joseph's in Philly made her a better offer." Bitterness lodged in his throat like a wad of gum. "And she also gave me some bull about not being suited for small-town life."

There was a beat of silence. "Did you really just curse? Wow. You must be pissed beyond belief."

Derek grabbed the Vernon file and stalked to the door. "Look, I need you to find out more about this St. Joseph's job. See if you can figure out how much they offered her—if it's a money thing, I might be able to match it."

Tate's whistle echoed in his ear. "You really want her, huh?"

Derek stiffened.

"As a nurse," Tate added, amusement ringing in his voice. "You must really want her as your nurse."

Derek neared the exam room. "I'm about to see a patient. Can you help or not, Tate?"

"I'm on it. I'll get back to you."

Derek disconnected the call and returned to Mrs. Vernon, spending the next twenty minutes reassuring her that she wasn't dying of any sort of conceivable disease. By the time he ushered her out of the room, he was ready to tear his hair out. Despite the packed waiting room, he told Nancy to give him a few minutes before sending in the next patient.

He stalked into his office, shut the door and let out a string of curses that no doubt would've stunned everyone in his family speechless.

Pacing the office, he thought of Amelia's agitated hazel eyes, the way she'd wrung her hands together and avoided his gaze. Then he remembered the way her entire face had lit up yesterday when he'd offered her a permanent position. How did a person go from happy to distressed in less than twenty-four hours?

Ask Tess.

Derek halted midstep. A jolt of pain shot through him as the memory of his wife surfaced, followed by a lump of bitterness that rose in his throat. Yeah, he knew all about irrational behavior, didn't he? The mood swings, the tears, the desperation. Tess's illness had destroyed their marriage—no matter how badly he'd wanted to be there for her, he hadn't been able to help the woman he loved.

Ignoring the painful throbbing in his chest, Derek took a deep breath and tried to clear his head. Christ. He couldn't hide out in his office thinking about Tess and Amelia. He had a responsibility to his patients and at the moment, that was all he could afford to concentrate on.

Several hours later, Derek bid goodbye to his last patient of the day, sent Nancy home and marched back to his office. He kept a change of clothes in a small cabinet by the door, and he shrugged out of his jacket as he headed for it. He ditched his scrubs and put on trousers and a cable-knit sweater, then shoved his feet into a pair of leather wing tips.

His cell phone rang just as he finished dressing. A glance at the caller ID revealed Tate's number. Finally.

"What'd you find out?" Derek asked in lieu of a greeting.

"Come outside and I'll tell you myself."

He wrinkled his forehead. "Why are you outside?"

"Because we've got Sawyer's parent-teacher thing in twenty minutes." Tate chuckled. "You forgot, didn't you?"

Busted.

Derek couldn't believe the conference had slipped his mind—he was normally on top of stuff like that. But Amelia's sudden departure had sent his mind reeling.

Damn. He'd been planning on heading straight to her apartment once he'd cleared his schedule, but Tate had thrown a wrench in that plan.

"I'll be out in a sec," he said as he grabbed the wool coat draped over the back of his desk chair.

Tate was waiting on the sidewalk in front of the clinic when Derek strode outside. After locking up and setting the alarm, Derek turned to his brother with an expectant look. "So? Did you get the information?"

Tate scrubbed a hand through his light brown hair. "Yeah, I did."

"What did St. Joseph's offer her?"

"Nothing."

Derek frowned. "What do you mean, nothing?"

"I mean, the human resources department at the hospital has never heard of Amelia Phillips. She never submitted a résumé, and she certainly didn't receive any job offers from them in the past twenty-four hours."

"You're certain of this?"

Tate nodded.

A fresh wave of frustration crashed into him. What the hell? Amelia had lied to him.

But why?

And if there was no offer from St. Joseph's, then what had spurred her to up and quit?

He shook his head. "I need to see her. Do you mind going to the school on your own?"

"No way, Doc." Tate's voice was firm. "We might all be Sawyer and Piper's guardians, but you're the one they look to as a father figure. And you're the one who stays on top of the school stuff. I need you there, bro."

Derek suppressed his annoyance. As much as he loved Tate, Gunnar and Emma, he sometimes felt as if they'd left him holding the bag after their parents died. Gunnar had enlisted in the military and disappeared for more than a decade, and although Tate and Emma had stuck around, they'd been more focused on their careers than their little siblings. And sure, their jobs in law enforcement were demanding, but so was Derek's practice. Why was *he* expected to juggle *his* work with the responsibility of raising two kids?

He'd never voice the complaint, though. He'd come to accept the reality of his situation—he was Derek, the responsible rock of the Colton family, the healer and protector, the man who always did the right thing, who always put others first. But sometimes he wished his siblings would step up and shoulder some of the burden. A man could bear only so much weight before he broke.

Sighing, he fished his car keys from his coat pocket. "We'll take separate cars. I want to head over to Amelia's the second the meeting ends."

Ten minutes later, he and Tate reconvened in the parking lot of Eden Falls Middle School. They entered the school through the back doors, their shoes squeaking against the linoleum floor as they made their way toward Sawyer's homeroom.

"So you're really riled up about Amelia," Tate remarked.

"She's a good nurse," he replied in a terse voice.

His brother's answering silence lasted far too long for his

liking. "What?" Derek said defensively. "Say what's on your mind, Tate."

Tate lifted his shoulders in a nonchalant pose. "Seems to me you're into more than her nursing abilities. You invited her to dinner—"

"Sawyer invited her," he cut in.

"And the private ranch tour? That was all you, Doc. You wanted to be alone with her."

He found himself unusually flustered. "That woman is damn secretive. I just wanted to get some answers."

As they approached Sawyer's classroom, Tate grabbed Derek's arm and forced him to stop. "It's okay to admit you like her," Tate said in quiet voice. "Tess has been gone for two years. It's about time you started to show interest in a woman."

Discomfort wrapped around his spine like strands of ivy. Tate was wrong. He didn't like Amelia, not in a romantic way, at least. He respected her. Appreciated her skills. Enjoyed her company.

Lusted over her gorgeous face and curvy body....

Shock spiraled through him. Holy crap. He *did* like her.

He shifted his gaze and noticed the barely restrained grin on his brother's face. "Just figuring it out now, huh?"

Derek promptly averted his eyes and took off in a brisk walk again. They reached Sawyer's classroom, but when he poked his head into the room, he saw that Sharon Bentley, Sawyer's teacher, hadn't wrapped up her current conference. She held up one hand to signal she'd be another five minutes.

Derek nodded in response, then stepped back into the hall and gestured to the wooden bench lining the wall. He and Tate sat, their big bodies awkwardly positioned on the kid-size bench. Both stood at six feet, and the bench was so low to the ground it was as if they were sitting on the floor.

"Anyway, about this Amelia thing," Tate continued.

"I can't talk about that right now. I...I can't." He let out a breath. "Tell me what's happening with the investigation."

Tate's expression hardened. "The sting operation is going down next week."

"So your informant came through?"

"Yeah, Miller's giving us the locations where the girls are being held. My supervisor has me posing as a buyer—I'm a rich New York businessman looking to buy myself a sex slave." A combination of revulsion and rage dripped from Tate's tone.

Derek felt pretty sick himself, and he was totally feeling his brother's rage, too. It horrified him to think that innocent girls were being sold off in a sex ring as if they were cattle. Both Tate and Emma were working overtime to crack this online ring wide open, and the coordinated efforts of the FBI and the Pennsylvania and Ohio PDs were finally paying off, especially now that Solomon Miller, a minor player in the ring, was working as an informant to help law enforcement nab the ringleaders.

"Gunnar's underwriting the op," Tate added, "so that'll make it easier to play the part of Richie Rich without costing the taxpayers a dime."

"What exactly does this sting op entail?" Derek asked.

"I'm going to *inspect the wares,*" Tate said in distaste. "As a buyer, I have the option to take a closer look at the girls before I commit to purchasing one."

Bile coated Derek's throat. "What happens if one of those girls is Hannah Troyer? Or Mary Yoder? Will your team swoop in and rescue them?"

To his shock, Tate shook his head. "Not during that first meeting."

"Jesus, Tate, why the hell not? You're just going to leave those girls at the hands of those sadistic bastards?"

"Our goal is to nail these sons of bitches to the wall," Tate said grimly. "Which means bringing down the ringleader and wiping out the entire ring. If we tip our hand now, the bastard will just close up shop or move the operation to some other state. We *will* rescue those girls, but not until the time is right."

"Dr. Colton? Detective Colton?"

Ms. Bentley's voice put an end to the conversation. Both men stood up as their brother's teacher appeared in front of them. "You can come in now," she said with a smile.

Before Derek could take a step, his phone went off. With an apologetic look, he fished out the phone. Although he was done for the day, he remained on call in the evenings.

"Give me a second," he said, gesturing for Tate to go with Sawyer's teacher.

Derek glanced at the caller ID and frowned when he saw the unknown number. He hoped this wasn't about Clara Watson—the woman had been having some complications with her latest pregnancy, and he'd already made three house calls to her in the past month, each time expecting the worst. He'd ordered her on bed rest, but he knew damn well that patients didn't always follow their doctor's orders.

"Dr. Colton," he barked as he flipped open the cell phone.

"Derek!"

His shoulders stiffened when Amelia's anguished voice sliced through the line.

"Amelia?" he said warily. "What's going on?"

"Oh, God, I…I… Can you come over?"

The terror in her tone was unmistakable and Derek's entire body went cold. "Are you okay?" he demanded. "Are you hurt?"

"Yes…no…please. Please, I need you."

"I'll be right there."

He hung up without another word, sprinted into the classroom and sought his brother's gaze. "I have to go," Derek said flatly.

Tate took one look at his face and paled. "Is it Sawyer? Piper?" He started to get up.

"They're fine," Derek said quickly. "It's a patient." He glanced at Ms. Bentley. "I apologize, Sharon, but I'm afraid you'll have to hold this conference without me."

Without letting either of them reply, Derek dashed out of the room. His heartbeat hammered out a frantic rhythm as he raced out of the school and hurried toward his car. He'd never heard Amelia sound like that. Panicked, shrill, frightened. His mind suddenly flashed to Tess, to the agitated voice mail she'd left him before she'd driven her car off that bridge.

His heart pounded even harder.

As he started the car and sped out of the parking lot, he prayed that Amelia was okay.

And that this time he wouldn't be too late.

Chapter 4

The first thing Derek saw when he approached apartment 203 was the smashed doorknob. Black marks marred the white paint of Amelia's door as if it had been scraped by something— a crowbar, perhaps—and wood splinters littered the weathered hardwood floor.

His entire body tensed, a jolt of adrenaline shuddering through him. "Amelia," he called as he burst through the door and entered the small apartment.

"In here."

He followed her muffled voice to the living room and found her huddled on the couch, her slender arms wrapped tightly around her knees. When she lifted her head, the tears gathering on her long lashes triggered a protective impulse. Dashing across the room, Derek yanked her to her feet and drew her into his arms. The sweet scent of honey and woman flooded his nostrils. Her blond hair tickled his chin as she buried her head in the crook of his neck, her tears staining his skin.

"What happened?" he demanded.

She pulled back and met his eyes. "Someone broke in," she answered in a tortured voice.

"Did you call the police?"

"No, I called you."

Bewilderment skated through him. "We need to call the

cops. Now." He let go of her abruptly. "The intruder might
still be in the—"

"There's nobody here," she interrupted. "I already checked."

"You checked?" he echoed. "Jesus, Amelia, you should've
run outside the second you saw the shape your door was in!"

The adrenaline in his blood spiked, mingling with the anger
pulsing in his veins. The foolish woman had come home to
find her doorknob smashed in and she'd stepped inside to investigate?

"Was anything stolen?" he asked, looking around the room.

An indecipherable expression flitted across her pretty face.
"I don't think so."

Sucking in a breath, he tried to calm the frantic beating of
his heart and fumbled in his coat pocket for his cell phone.
"I'm calling the cops."

"No."

Her fearful interjection caught him off guard. "What do you
mean no? Someone broke into your apartment, sweetheart. We
need to report the break-in."

"No."

Derek resisted the urge to rip his hair out. What was wrong
with her? Why was she—

He froze, noticing the wild look in her hazel eyes. The way
her entire body trembled like a leaf being blown around by a
gust of wind. The tears streaming down her cheeks.

And then she started babbling.

"I can't call the police, Derek. I can't. I'll have to fill out
a report and then there'll be an official record and then Fe—
whoever broke in will know for sure that I'm—" Her breath
came out in rapid pants. "I fixed the door today! I thought
it would be enough and then I realized it *wasn't* enough and
I...I..."

As she trailed off, her body went still, her expression taking on a blank stare.

Fingers of uneasiness clawed up Derek's spine. Oh, Christ.

Her hysteria, the odd behavior, the crazy talk. Her constant nervousness and secretive nature. He'd seen and heard it all before, and he couldn't believe he hadn't recognized the signs after spending ten years with a woman who suffered from a mental illness.

As he looked into Amelia's expressionless eyes, he suddenly remembered all the "false alarms" Tess had put him through—calling him in a panic and claiming it was an emergency, and then when he rushed home, he'd find her sitting on the couch with that same deadened look Amelia wore now.

Softening his tone, Derek planted both hands on Amelia's delicate shoulders and fixed her with a gentle look. "Maybe I should take you to the hospital."

Chloe's head jerked up. "What?" she said in shock.

"It's clear that you're shaken up," Derek went on in a voice reserved for small children and skittish animals. "And I think it might be helpful to get checked out, maybe talk to a medical profess—"

"A shrink?" she interrupted, snapping out of the fear-induced trance she'd gone into when she'd come home from the bank and discovered yet another break-in. "I don't need to see a shrink, Derek."

But he clearly thought she did, and Chloe realized she couldn't blame him for thinking her unstable. She'd been acting like a crazy person from the second he'd walked through the door. Of course he'd think she was nuts.

She dragged both hands through her hair, battling a rush of frustration, fighting the ripples of fear that continued to plague her body.

She had no doubt that Felix had been responsible for the break-in. Thankfully, she'd been out when he'd decided to pay her another visit. After quitting her job, she'd spent the day running errands. She'd purchased the supplies she needed to sustain her on the road. Emptied her bank account in town.

Called her contact so he could get the ball rolling on a new identity. She'd planned on hitting the road tonight, but when she returned home and found Felix's present, she'd panicked, plain and simple.

And her first instinct had been to call Derek.

"I am shaken up," she relented, exhaling a calming breath. "But only because my apartment was just broken into. I'm scared and I freaked out, but I assure you, I'm not having some sort of breakdown right now."

He still looked dubious. "Then why not call the police?"

"Because..." She scanned her brain for a logical excuse. "Because I know who broke in."

His dark eyebrows rose. "You do?"

"Yes."

"Who?"

Chloe hesitated. Somehow, in the past three weeks, she'd come to trust Derek Colton. She'd known without a shred of doubt that he would come to her aid when she called, and he hadn't proved her wrong. But the way he was looking at her now, with those troubled brown eyes, told her that he was far too intelligent, far too perceptive, to buy any lies she sold him.

So tell him the truth.

Fear trickled through her. The truth? No. She couldn't.

"Okay," Derek said after her silence dragged on too long. "I think it's time to get the police involved."

Her pulse raced. "No. Please. I don't want to do that."

"Why the hell not? Damn it, Amelia, tell me what's going on."

The lethal edge in his voice made her flinch. She'd never seen Derek look so angry, and she instinctively backed away from him, an irrational part of her expecting him to strike her.

He must have seen the fear in her eyes because shock flooded his handsome face. "Don't look at me like that," he said in a firm voice. "I am *not* going to hurt you, sweetheart. I'm trying to help, damn it."

Wow. Two *damns* in less than a minute. Derek hardly ever cursed. He must really be upset with her.

Tell him the truth, the little voice repeated.

Biting on her lower lip, Chloe stared into his frustrated eyes, wanting so badly to trust him. But how could she? How was she supposed to admit that she'd been lying to him from the moment they'd met?

"I can't do this," Derek mumbled, edging away from her. "I'm leaving, Amelia. I'll call the police and wait downstairs until they show up."

She watched in dismay as he headed for the doorway. "Derek—"

He kept walking.

"It was my husband!" she burst out.

That broad back stiffened.

Very slowly, he turned around and sought out her eyes. The surprise etched into his features was unmistakable. "What?"

"My husband," she said in a dull voice. "That's who broke in."

He shook his head repeatedly, as if trying to make sense of that. "Your husband."

She nodded, her shoulders sagging with defeat. "Yes."

"You're married."

"Yes. Well, kind of."

"Kind of?" A humorless laugh popped out of his mouth. "What the hell does that mean?"

"It means that it's a very long story," she answered, releasing a heavy sigh. "One that probably needs to be told over a drink. Or ten." She took a step toward the kitchen. "Have a seat. I'll get the whiskey."

Chloe hurried out of the room before he could object, but she knew he wouldn't go anywhere. The bomb she'd dropped in his lap was too big to ignore.

She found a bottle of Maker's Mark in the cupboard over the sink, grabbed two plastic cups then stood in the middle of the small kitchen, breathing deeply. Could she really do this? Confide in Derek? Tell him all the pathetic, sordid details of her miserable life?

And once she did, what could Derek really do? Help her disappear? Get rid of Felix for her? That was unlikely on both counts.

Yet even though she knew spilling her guts to Derek wouldn't achieve a damn thing—except provoke his pity, perhaps—she felt compelled to tell him the truth. She might be leaving town, but Derek deserved to know the truth before she left. He'd been unbelievably kind to her these past three weeks and she couldn't in good conscience disappear from his life without at least telling him why she was doing it.

Derek's mind continued to reel as he waited for Amelia to return. Amelia was *married*?

Kind of, he amended, whatever the hell *that* meant. And why had this "kind of" husband broken into her apartment?

The situation had trouble written all over it, yet he couldn't bring himself to leave. After weeks of trying to solve the puzzle that was Amelia Phillips, she was giving him the answers he craved, willingly providing him with the puzzle pieces he'd been unable to fit together.

As Amelia strode back into the living room, he instantly noticed the change in her demeanor—eyes devoid of tears, shoulders straight, head high. She looked as if she were walking into battle, armed with a bottle of whiskey, two cups and— was that a *wedding dress*?

His gaze snagged on the poofy white garment tucked under her left arm. "What's that?"

With a resigned expression, she set the bottle and cups on the coffee table, then held up the dress for him to see. He recoiled when she turned the dress to give him a frontal view. Why the hell were the bodice and full skirt stained red? Not bright crimson, but a dark reddish-brown that resembled… blood.

She stepped closer, and his nostrils flared as a metallic scent wafted in his direction.

Derek's gaze flew to hers. "Why is that dress covered with blood, Amelia?"

She gulped. "It was like this when I found it."

"You found it," he repeated.

"Hanging in the closet. And before you ask, I didn't hang it there." Her fingers trembled, causing the lacy material to crinkle. "I left this dress behind when I escaped six months ago."

Escaped. Her choice of word didn't go unnoticed. Wariness circled his stomach, deepening when he glimpsed the weary look in Amelia's eyes.

"But now the dress is here, in my apartment, stained with blood." She placed the dress on the armchair opposite the couch. "I doubt it's human blood. Or if it is, it probably came from a blood bank and not some innocent person Felix murdered in order to send his sick message."

"Felix." Derek frowned. "That's your husband?"

Nodding, she joined him on the sofa and leaned forward to untwist the cap of the whiskey bottle. She splashed the amber-colored liquid into each glass, then handed him one.

Derek brought the cup to his lips and took a small sip. He was on call, but one drink wouldn't hurt. The whiskey burned a fiery path down to his gut, soothing his addled brain.

Next to him, Amelia threw her head back and downed the whiskey. She made a face, then poured herself another glass. She sucked that back, too, before turning to face him. "My name isn't Amelia Phillips, Derek."

He blinked in surprise.

"It's Chloe Moreno," she confessed, a note of sorrow in her voice. "Six months ago I faked my own suicide."

His mouth fell open.

"It sounds crazy, but it's true." A desperate laugh flew out of her mouth. "I crashed our plane into the ocean." Another burst of laughter. "Everyone I know thinks my body is at the bottom of the Pacific. They even threw me a memorial service and everything."

It took a moment for Derek's brain to start functioning again. He stared at Amelia—no, Chloe. He stared at *Chloe* in sheer disbelief. "You faked your death. Why?"

"Because if I didn't, my husband would have killed me," she said simply.

He kept staring, unable to decide whether he should believe her. Her story was…unbelievable. Absurd. Yet her face was dead serious, which either made her a phenomenal actress, or this tale of hers was absurd enough to be true.

"Felix is a dangerous man," Chloe whispered. "He's a sick man. Controlling, ruthless, violent."

Derek slugged back the rest of his whiskey. "Jesus, Amel—Chloe, please don't tell me you're some gangster's moll."

"Try a plastic surgeon's trophy wife," she replied wryly.

He faltered. "No way."

"It's true. I married Felix when I was twenty-nine. Back then I thought he truly loved me, but it turned out all he loved was the idea of me. A pretty, wealthy socialite he could mold and manipulate. The perfect little Stepford Wife for his perfect little life. He kept up a good act for the first few years of our marriage, but after that…well, he stopped trying to hide who he was."

"And who was he?" Derek asked roughly.

"A maniac." Her pulse jumped in her throat. "And again, before you ask, there were a lot of reasons why I didn't leave him."

He hadn't been going to ask, but he didn't correct her. The second Amelia—Chloe—had uttered the word *violent* in her description of her husband, Derek had finally understood the reason behind the shadows that haunted her hazel eyes. The reason for her skittishness, her secretive nature, the way she shied away from unsolicited physical contact.

This woman had been abused. Repeatedly. And for years. It all made sense now, and as a physician, Derek knew better than to ask why Chloe hadn't left her husband long before now. Abusive spouses had ways of maintaining their power and control over their victims. They used guilt, fear, shame, threats—anything they could to wear down their spouse and trap them in a situation that eventually seems impossible to escape.

"At first I blamed myself for Felix's actions," Chloe admitted, resting her glass on her knee and fingering the rim. "I don't want to get into it, but we were going through a lot of issues, and as messed up as this sounds, I thought I deserved what was happening to me. I felt like I'd let him down in so many ways, and when he told me I was a failure, that I was defective, I believed him."

Derek's heart clenched. Despite himself, he set his glass on the table and reached for her hand. Her skin was cold, clammy, and he rubbed her knuckles, trying to warm her.

"That's not uncommon," he said gently. "There's an astounding number of reasons why people remain in abusive situations. Often times the abused partner will rationalize the abuser's actions, tell themselves that it's their fault for upsetting their spouse."

"I was an emotional basket case," she confessed, sounding ashamed. "At the beginning Felix preferred verbal abuse to physical, but then one day he got angry about something and hit me. A backhand to the face. I was stunned, but I—" Her face collapsed. "I made excuses for it. Once the violence became more regular, I realized I couldn't let it keep happening. I was already suffering from depression thanks to—" She halted "—to those issues I don't want to get into. I started seeing a therapist and she made me see that the beatings weren't my fault and that I didn't deserve a single second of what was happening. Not long after, I found the courage to tell Felix that our marriage was over."

Derek held his breath, knowing the story wouldn't end there.

"He freaked out. A divorce would have ruined his perfect image, but I think it was more than that—he loved having power over me, having a little toy he could play with and toss around whenever he felt like it. He told me that he owned me and that he would never let me go. When I told him I'd file for divorce, anyway, he beat me so badly I could barely move for days—and then he threatened to kill my father."

The breath came out in a sharp puff. "What?"

"I was telling the truth about my dad's illness," Chloe said, shooting him an imploring look. "He does live in a facility in St. Louis, he does suffer from dementia and he's the only family I have."

"Why didn't you tell the police about the threat?"

"I did," she said flatly. "I went to the station and filed a report. When the detective I spoke to brought Felix in, my husband did what he does best—manipulated the situation. When I tried to show them the bruises from the beating, he pulled out a bogus medical report saying I fell down the stairs and a signed statement from our housekeeper backing up the story. Then he gave the cops this whole speech about how mentally unbalanced I was. He had documents from my psychiatrist to back it up, showed them my antidepressant medication, pretty much made me look like a crazy person. Then he dragged me home and threatened to kill me if I ever tried something like that again."

"What did you do?"

She let out a heavy breath. "I went home with him and tried to figure out my next move. First thing, I took my dad out of the Malibu facility he was in and moved him to a home in St. Louis, which was where we lived before my parents moved us to Beverly Hills when I was five. I specifically arranged it so that I was his only approved visitor and the only one able to make decisions about his care."

Bitterness dripped from her voice. "And Felix, of course, proved that no matter what I did, he'd be able to get to my dad. His first week at the new facility, Felix paid my father a visit, showed the staff a forged letter from me granting him access to his father-in-law, and what do you know, Dad had an 'accident' while walking with Felix on the grounds. He broke his leg and was bedridden for two months."

Derek squeezed her hand tighter. His heart ached for her, and he knew from the tortured look in her eyes and raw pain in her voice that every word she spoke was the truth.

"So I resigned myself to my fate." She sighed. "I continued my charity work, tried to stay out of Felix's way, played the part of the perfect wife when we were in public together. He stopped beating me, but he was just as vicious verbally and just as controlling. And then…"

She fell silent abruptly.

Derek reached out and grasped her chin, angling her head to force eye contact. "And then what?"

"He killed someone I cared about." A shaky breath left her mouth. "I was heading up a charity committee and I became close with my co-chair. He was smart, handsome, funny."

"And you had an affair with him," Derek finished in a gentle tone.

"No." She smiled. "He was gay. But we did become friends." The smile faded. "When Felix found out, he jumped to the same the conclusion you just did and accused me of having an affair. I denied it, he didn't believe me. He forced me to quit the committee, and two weeks later my co-chair was found dead in an underground parking garage in L.A."

"Are you certain Felix killed him?" Derek asked sharply.

"He bragged about it," she said with an angry shake of her head. "He said I belonged to him and that the same thing that happened to Jim would happen to the next man I got chummy with. There was no evidence to link Felix to Jim's death, but I know he had him killed, Derek. I just know it."

"Is that what drove you to finally leave?"

After a beat of hesitation, she nodded.

An alarm went off in his head, triggering a bout of suspicion. He got the feeling that she'd left out an important part of the story, but he didn't want to push her. Now that her story was winding down, she looked ready to bolt, but he wasn't letting her go anywhere, not until he got some more answers.

"When you applied for a job at the clinic...were those documents you gave me forgeries?" he asked with an edge to his voice. "The résumé, the nursing license, the recommendation letters?"

Her eyes widened. "No, they were real. I do have a nursing degree, I did earn a psychology degree from Berkeley and I did work for eight years at the hospital in L.A." Shame crossed her face. "Only the name on those documents was a lie."

"How did you swing that?"

"I know someone who deals with identity papers," she admitted. "I met him while volunteering at the hospital. He used to work in army intelligence and has a lot of contacts. He was expensive but worth it. He created an entire life for Amelia Phillips—birth certificate, Social Security number, medical records. Because I'd attended Berkeley as Chloe Moreno, he created a new record for Amelia Phillips using my actual grades and transcripts, same with my employment records. And once I left California, I took the examination in Missouri to renew my license, just like I wrote that same exam last week so I could practice in Pennsylvania."

"You convinced me to hire you under false pretenses," he said bitterly.

She swallowed. "Under a false name. But my training is real, and so is my skill. I'm a damn good nurse, Derek. Think what you want of me, but you can't deny that I'm good at my job."

"You are good." He met her eyes. "But what now, Ame—

Chloe? Your cover has been blown. Your husband knows you're alive. What are you planning to do now?"

"Run."

Alarm shot through him. "What are you talking about?"

"I can't stay in Eden Falls. That's why I quit today. I need to get out of town as soon as I can."

"That's crazy," he said firmly. "You can't keep running."

"What other choice do I have?"

"Call the cops, and tell them about Felix."

She lifted her chin in fortitude. "No. If I do that, he'll hurt my father."

"Not if you tell them about the threat to your father. The police can arrange round-the-clock protection for him."

"And who will protect me?" she countered. "Don't kid your-self—Felix *will* kill me. He'll kill me and make it look like an accident, or use his powerful connections to cover it up."

"What kind of connections can he possibly have? You said he was a doctor—" Derek halted as something clicked.

Felix Moreno.

Christ, even he knew who Felix Moreno was, and he was just a small-town doctor from Pennsylvania Dutch country. Moreno was a renowned plastic surgeon, one of the best in the world, not to mention the author of dozens of studies, a highly sought-after consultant, a personal friend of several senators and a frequent visitor to the White House.

He scanned his brain, trying to remember what he'd heard about Moreno's wife, but he came up blank. All he knew was that the celebrity surgeon had married a socialite.

A trophy wife, as Chloe had said.

"You get it now, don't you?" she murmured.

He grimaced. "Yeah, I get it."

"Felix will go to great lengths to protect his reputation. He'll kill me and everyone I love before risking people know-ing that he's a wife beater."

Derek dragged a hand over his scalp, the short bristles of

his hair scraping his palm. "So you're simply going to disappear again? Buy yourself a new identity and hope that Felix doesn't track you down this time?"

"Yes."

"And what about your father? If Felix knows you're alive, who's to stop him from using your father to lure you out of hiding?"

Chloe paled. "Oh, God."

Feeling like an ass for scaring her, Derek touched her cheek again. "We'll hire a guard for your dad. One call to Tate and there'll be a bodyguard posted outside your father's door by tomorrow morning. And in the meantime, we'll go to the police."

She responded with that stubborn shake of the head again. "No. Even if I did, Felix wouldn't go to jail. All he did was send a few wedding mementos—he probably wouldn't even get charged for that. I won't go to the cops. Not until I figure out what to do. I need a couple of days to think things through."

His jaw tensed. "There's no way you're staying in this apartment one second longer." His gaze strayed to the blood-covered wedding dress on the armchair. "If Felix makes a move, you're a sitting duck here."

She opened her mouth, but he held up his hand to silence her. "You're coming back to the Double C with me. Tonight."

"No way," she said swiftly. "I won't bring this trouble to your doorstep. I don't want him breaking into your home and hurting anyone in your family."

"The ranch has a top-notch security system." He glanced pointedly around her small apartment. "This place, however, doesn't. Your life is in danger and I'm not leaving you alone. So suck it up—you're coming home with me."

"I can't—"

"Yes you can," he interrupted, his tone brooking no argument. With a burst of determination, he stumbled to his feet, pulling her up with him. "Pack a bag, Amel—Chloe. I'm getting you out of here."

"Why?" she whispered, fixing those big hazel eyes on his face. "Why would you do this for me?"

"Because I don't want to see you hurt. Because I want to help you. Because I took an oath to save lives. Take your pick."

A wry smile lifted her lush mouth. "I don't think there's anything in the Hippocratic oath about taking in a woman who's running from her psycho husband."

"Sure there is. It's in the footnotes."

She laughed, and the melodic sound warmed his heart. Then her expression turned serious. "Are you sure you want to do this? I have a lot of baggage, Derek. I won't be upset or insulted if you don't want to get involved."

"I have a lot of baggage, too," he said hoarsely. "And a big house, so there's plenty of room for both our baggage. You can stay for a few days and I'll help you figure out your next move."

Their eyes locked, and despite the graveness of the situation, Derek experienced a flicker of heat. Amelia Phillips, Chloe Moreno, whatever name she called herself—it didn't matter, and it didn't change the way his body reacted to her nearness. She was so achingly beautiful that he wanted to pull her into his arms and kiss her senseless. He wanted to stroke her silky skin and cup those firm breasts and run his hands over every inch of her curvy body.

Inappropriate much?

Shoving away the unwelcome images, Derek cleared his throat. "Grab your things. It's time to go."

Chapter 5

Chloe swept her gaze around Derek's living room, surprised by how cozy it was. She'd expected a more sterile atmosphere, considering the minimalist decorating style of Derek's office at the clinic, but this room exuded warmth and elegance. Brown leather couches set up in an L-shape graced one side of the space, while the other side boasted tall bookshelves crammed with everything from medical texts to romance novels. She couldn't picture Derek relaxing with a romance, so she figured those must have belonged to Derek's wife, whose feminine presence could be seen in the room. The yellow curtains hanging by the large bay window spoke of a woman's touch, as did the pink-and-peach decorative pillows arranged on the sofas.

But there were no photographs of Tess in the room, and when she'd sneaked a peek into the master bedroom and glimpsed the black-and-gray color scheme, a total contrast from the peach-and-gold of the guest bedrooms, she suspected that Derek had redecorated his room after Tess died. Was it because he couldn't bear falling asleep in a room that reminded him of his wife?

As she lingered in the doorway, Chloe realized that Derek had yet to mention the mysterious Tess to her. She could hardly fault him, though. She hadn't exactly mentioned *her* husband, either, at least prior to tonight.

"You want something to eat?"

Derek's voice made her jump. She turned as he came up beside her. "No, thank you. I don't have much of an appetite."

And the whiskey she'd consumed back at her apartment was burning a hole in her belly, making her feel queasy. She wasn't much of a drinker, but she'd definitely needed the liquid courage earlier.

"Let's sit down," he suggested.

After they settled on the couch, Chloe met his somber, chocolate-brown eyes and felt a spark of unease. While she'd gotten changed in the guest room, Derek had been on the phone, but she hadn't been able to make out what he was saying. Judging from his expression, his phone call must have been serious.

"What's wrong?" she asked immediately.

"Nothing's wrong," he assured her. "But I do have to go in a few minutes to meet Tate. I'm giving him the dress so he can test the blood. And before you argue, I want you to know Tate gave me his word that he wouldn't involve anyone at the police department. He has a friend at a private lab in Philly and she'll test the sample on the down low."

Chloe nodded, relieved. "That's fine. But I still don't think it's human blood. Felix wouldn't leave behind anything that might incriminate him in something illegal, particularly a murder."

"I'd still feel better knowing for sure," Derek said firmly.

"Okay." She cocked her head. "Is that all?"

"I asked Tate to arrange a bodyguard for your father—everything will be in place tomorrow morning. And in the meantime, I phoned the facility and spoke to the doctor in charge of your father's case. Your dad is safe. He's sleeping comfortably in his room."

Gratitude tugged at her heart. God, this man was so wonderful, sometimes she wondered if she'd dreamed him up. "Thank you," she whispered.

"You're welcome," he said gruffly, then cleared his throat.

"Also, I'm sending one of my ranch hands to fix your door in the morning."

They'd already decided not to call her landlady, Greta, who was on vacation for the next three weeks. Chloe had opted to fix the door herself. That way she wouldn't have to tell Greta about the break-in and risk the woman reporting it to the cops.

"I can hire someone to do it," Chloe answered.

"It's no problem. I'll take care of it."

"No. I won't have you sending one of your employees to take care of my mess. You've already done so much—I can't let you pay to have my door fixed."

He shot her a stubborn look. "Tough. I'm doing it. And the money isn't an issue."

"It's not an issue for me, either," she muttered. "I just don't want to take advantage of you."

He ignored the last remark and focused on the previous one. "Money's not a problem, huh?" His eyes twinkled. "Did you pilfer Felix's accounts before you left?"

She sighed. "Actually, I sold off some jewelry."

He wrinkled his brows.

"I couldn't touch the inheritance I got from my parents," she explained. "Felix has access to that account, and he would've been suspicious if a chunk of cash disappeared right before my supposed death."

The jewelry had been a safer bet, and fortunately, Felix had bought her an obscene amount of it over the years. He would never notice if some of the pieces were missing, and Chloe had cashed in more than half a million dollars' worth of jewels before her suicide.

They fell silent, and she could tell Derek was mulling over the details she'd given him. Yet he didn't seem to be judging her. He'd confessed on the drive to the ranch that he'd offered his medical services to several women's shelters during his residency, so she suspected he had some experience with abused women.

The label made her cringe. Abused woman. It seemed surreal, calling herself that, especially when she'd always believed herself to be a strong and capable individual. If someone had told her when she was younger that she'd end up at the mercy of a violent man, she would've laughed. Nobody liked to think that something like that could happen to them.

Her hand unconsciously moved to rub her left cheek, a reminder of what her fate could've been if she hadn't gotten out when she had.

"So you crashed a plane, huh?"

Derek's bemused remark drew her from her thoughts. When she met his gaze, she saw a combination of curiosity and admiration glimmering there.

"I took flying lessons for six months," she admitted. "Felix thought I was heading up a charity for underprivileged children, which I was, except the weekly committee meetings didn't take the two hours I claimed. For that second hour, I was up in the sky. I learned to fly on a Cessna, the same model as our plane, which was what I flew the morning I 'died.'"

He looked alarmed. "Please don't tell me you were in the plane when it went down."

"I parachuted out before the plane even reached the ocean. The autopilot did the rest."

"I never took you for a skydiver."

She shrugged. "Trust me, I'm the furthest thing from an adrenaline junkie, but it was the only way I could get out. I knew there couldn't be a body, but I had to convince Felix I was truly gone. The friend I mentioned before also helped me come up with the exit plan."

"You're full of surprises, aren't you?" he murmured.

She had to smile. "All bad ones, I suspect."

Derek searched her face. "Why take such a huge risk, Chloe? What would've happened if your plan didn't go off as smoothly as it did?"

"It was a risk I was willing to take. I had to get out, Derek. I figured I would either get away with it and live, or screw it up and die." A lump rose in her throat. "Either way, I'd be free."

Either way I'd be free.

Chloe's words continued to haunt Derek as he parked his car in front of his brother Gunnar's cabin, which was located on the far edge of the Double C. He couldn't believe how courageous the woman was. She'd taken a monumental risk when she'd faked her death and escaped her husband, yet the danger hadn't stopped her from carrying through with her plans. And when she'd recited her story, she'd been so calm, exuding an inner strength that had awed him.

He didn't particularly agree with her decision to keep the cops out of this, but he understood where it stemmed from. Felix Moreno had tormented Chloe for years, and though she put on a brave face, Derek knew she still feared her husband. Breaking the cycle of fear and abuse didn't happen overnight. Chloe had taken a big step toward self-healing, but Derek suspected a part of her still viewed herself as the powerless, "defective" woman Moreno had labeled her so many years ago.

Getting out of the car, Derek tucked the garbage bag that held Chloe's bloody dress under his arm and climbed the wooden steps of Gunnar's porch. Tate's sedan was already parked on the dirt next to Gunnar's Suburban.

He found both his brothers in Gunnar's den, hunched over a laptop as they murmured to one another.

"All set," Gunnar said, keying in a few strokes. "The money's been transferred to a numbered account in the Caymans. Whenever you're ready, you can reroute it to whatever account you'll be using for your cover story."

"Great. I owe you one, bro."

"Hey, what's the fun in being a billionaire if you can't share the wealth?"

Derek hid a smile. Just hearing the word *billionaire* made his head spin. The Colton family was well off, but Gunnar had taken that wealth to a new level when several prudent invest-ments had skyrocketed while he'd been serving in the mili-tary. Gunnar had returned home from the service to discover he was officially filthy rich, and though he was still the same gruff and crabby eldest Colton, his siblings never failed to tease him about his new status.

"Quit lurking and come in, Doc," Gunnar called, humor ringing in his voice.

Derek wasn't surprised that his brother had sensed his pres-ence even with his back turned to the door. Gunnar was always aware of everything and everyone around him, thanks to his military training. The guy's instincts were spot-on.

"So you're all set for the undercover op?" Derek asked Tate as he strode into the den.

"Yep." Tate's jaw hardened. "We're going to crack this sex ring wide open."

"Good." Derek's own jaw tensed as he held up the bag con-taining Chloe's wedding dress. "Here's the dress I mentioned. It needs to be tested ASAP."

"You sure it's blood?"

"Looks and smells like it." He set the bag on the small cre-denza by the door, then settled in one of the leather armchairs across from Gunnar's desk. "Amelia—well, it's Chloe, actu-ally—she's freaking out about this. Which brings me to the next favor I need from you."

While Gunnar closed his laptop and leaned back in his chair, Tate flopped down in the second armchair. "What is it?"

"I want you to do some digging about Felix Moreno. Back-ground check, financial statements. Oh, and his current loca-tion. Chloe is convinced Felix is here in town, and considering the items that were left at her place, I'm inclined to agree. But I'd like to be sure."

"Done. Anything else?"

"Just make sure you're discreet. I don't want to tip the bas-tard off that anyone's asking about him. And I don't want anyone outside our family knowing that Chloe is staying at my place." He gave a grim look. "In fact, you two and Emma are the only ones who can know her real name. Call her Amelia when you're around Piper and Sawyer, or—" he glanced at Gunnar "—even Violet."

When Gunnar and Tate exchanged a look, Derek's spine stiffened. "What?" he said defensively.

After a second of hesitation, Gunnar ran his hand over his stubble-dotted jaw. "What are you doing, Doc?"

"What do you mean?"

"Inviting this woman into your home, hiring a guard for her father, gathering intel about her husband. Her *husband*. She's married, Derek." Gunnar's forehead creased. "You're going to a lot of trouble to help her, and you barely even know her. So why?"

Damn good question. In fact, he'd been asking himself that very same thing ever since he'd brought Chloe back to his place. It was in his nature to help people, but deep down he knew his decision to take Chloe in was about more than simply being a Good Samaritan.

The woman had gotten under his skin from the moment they'd met. She was beautiful. Intelligent. Kindhearted. She also happened to be the first woman to snag his interest since Tess's death.

The first woman in two years to call to something deep and primal inside him.

"She's in danger," he muttered. "She needs someone to look out for her."

"And it has to be you?" Gunnar countered.

Tate suddenly laughed. "Of course it has to be him," he told Gunnar. "This is Mr. Perfect we're talking about. The gallant knight who slays dragons and rescues damsels."

Derek frowned. "Is that really how you see me?"

Tate's expression sobered. "Hey, now, I wasn't making fun of you. I'm damn proud of you, Doc, and I respect the hell out of you. You're a lot like Dad in that sense—larger than life, always stepping in and saving the day, keeping a cool head when everything falls apart."

The comparison to their father brought a twinge of pain to his heart. Donovan Colton had been widely respected in the community, the man everyone turned to when they needed help or advice, or hell, even just a cup of coffee with a friend. Growing up, Derek had strived to be like his adoptive father, to master that same patience, develop that same strength and determination. Most days he thought he'd succeeded in following in his old man's footsteps. Other days, he felt like a fraud, particularly when he thought about Tess.

Where had his patience been then? He'd tried to be understanding, tried to help her work through her inner struggles, but it hadn't been enough. He'd failed.

Donovan Colton wouldn't have failed.

"Chloe needs me," Derek said in a rough voice. "She wouldn't have asked me for help if she hadn't been desperate. I know how hard it was for her to confide in me, which is why I can't let her down."

"How long do you plan on playing house?" Gunnar asked warily.

He shrugged. "Until she decides what she wants to do. A few days probably. But I don't want her making any rash decisions and skipping town until we have more information about who broke into her apartment."

"Well, I'll do my best with that," Tate said, rising from the armchair. He crossed the room and grabbed the bag Derek had dropped off. "I'll get this tested, and in the meantime I'll see what I can find out about Moreno. I'll be staying at my place in Philly until I leave for New York, so call if you need anything else."

"Thanks," Derek said gratefully. He stood up, glancing from one brother to the other. "I know neither of you is crazy about this situation. Trust me, I'm not thrilled about it, either. But I can't turn Chloe away. I promised I'd help her."

No, he *needed* to help her. But he couldn't voice the thought. Neither Tate nor Gunnar suspected just how deeply his guilt ran. How he lay in bed at night, tormented, agonizing about Tess and all the things he could have done differently. All the ways he could have tried harder to help his wife.

He hadn't been able to help Tess, but he sure as hell could help Chloe.

And this time, Derek refused to fail.

In the presidential suite of the Philadelphia Hilton, Felix Moreno stood by the floor-to-ceiling windows and examined the people bustling on the sidewalk below. From his vantage point, those people looked like ants. Little ants crawling along, going about their day, doing whatever mediocre things mediocre people did. A smirk lifted his lips. He had the urge to crush those ants with the toe of his Gucci loafer.

Turning away from the unimpressive display of easily forgotten people, he strode across the expensive carpet toward the mahogany desk in the suite's sitting area. He lowered his Armani-clad body into the leather chair and scrolled through the saved text messages in his BlackBerry, searching for the confirmation details about tomorrow night's appointment.

Once he reread the message, he opened his photo app and brought up a picture of his wife.

Chloe's big hazel eyes stared up at him, wrought with vulnerability. Her dark blond hair was loose, cascading over one shoulder, her cupid's-bow mouth pursed in a tiny smile.

As usual, a barrage of emotions swarmed his body at the sight of his wife's face. Fury. Disappointment. Sorrow. Love. Disgust. How one little woman could inspire so many big, conflicting emotions was a downright mystery.

He stared at the photograph, studied it, but the answers he sought didn't come.

"You stupid bitch," he muttered. "You stupid, stupid bitch."

Would it have killed her to try harder? To do more to please him? To obey him the way she'd promised in their wedding vows?

He'd given Chloe everything she'd ever wanted, and all he'd expected in return was love and obedience. Fidelity and respect. He could have married anyone he wanted, but he'd chosen *her*. One would think she'd have shown more gratitude.

The ringing of his phone jarred him from his angry thoughts. When he saw the caller ID, a combination of pleasure and apprehension shuddered through his blood.

"Hello, Mother," he answered.

He held his breath as he awaited her response. He could always decipher her mood based on the tone of her voice.

"Hello, darling."

Cool, precise, hard.

Panic fluttered up his spine. She was unhappy with him.

"Why did I have to find out from your secretary that you're out of town?" Bianca Moreno asked coldly.

"I know. I'm sorry," Felix said quickly. "It was a last-minute thing, Mother. I was planning on calling you when I got in."

"And are you in?"

"Yes."

"Then why was I the one who phoned you?"

His palms grew damp. "I walked into my suite just as you rang. I literally had the phone in my hand, about to call you."

"Is that true, Felix?"

"Yes," he lied.

When her voice relaxed, so did his shoulders. "That pleases me, then. How was the flight, darling?"

"Uneventful." He rose from the chair and headed back to the windows.

"Did you order an in-flight meal?"

"Yes. The vegetarian dish."

"Good, that's good, darling. I'm happy you're reducing your red meat intake like we discussed."

Relief rippled in his stomach. Bianca Moreno was not the easiest woman to love—high maintenance, easily offended, with impossible standards at times. But she lived to make her son happy, and as a young boy he'd known that bringing her that same happiness in return would be his life's goal. He'd recently turned fifty-one, but his devotion to the woman who'd borne and raised him had not dimmed. There was only one woman he trusted in his life, only one woman who had never let him down, only one woman who put him above all else.

Chloe had mocked him about it. Accused him of being unable to stand up to his mother. The bitch hadn't understood that standing up to Bianca was unnecessary because his mother always had their best interests at heart. She'd even moved into their home to help Chloe, but had his wife thanked his mother for it? Not once.

"Now, how long will this trip take?" Bianca inquired.

"A few days, Mother. I have got several appointments to meet and a patient who requires my assistance."

"As do I, darling. You promised you'd take care of that wrinkle for me."

She sounded annoyed again, and he quickly attempted to soothe her. "I will clear my schedule the day I return and take care of that injection for you, Mother. But we both know you don't need it. You're more beautiful than any of the young starlets who walk into my office."

Bianca giggled. "I am, aren't I? Seventy-two years old yet you'd never know it. What age do you think I pass for, darling?"

He gave her the standard answer, the one that never failed to make her smile. "Forty-eight, of course."

"Thanks to my handsome, talented son." Bianca laughed again. "Now, I must run, darling. I have a nail appointment in twenty minutes. Please phone me this evening."

"I will, Mother."

They said goodbye and disconnected, Felix's gaze once again focusing on the pedestrians bustling along the sidewalk thirty-five stories below. Philadelphia really was a dull place. Could hardly even be considered a city when compared to the modern, glittering hub that was Los Angeles. The East Coast bored Felix—too cold, too bland, too pedestrian. He supposed Newport and the Hamptons were tolerable, but nothing outshone the glamour of the West.

Good thing he wouldn't be here long. Only a few pesky business matters to deal with, and then he'd be sipping champagne in the cabin of his chartered jet, on his way home to his beachfront mansion and booming practice.

He clicked a button on his phone and summoned Chloe's picture again, frowning as he stared into those familiar hazel eyes.

"You ungrateful bitch," he murmured.

Then he shoved the phone in his pocket and headed for the door.

Chapter 6

By the time Derek came home at six o'clock the next evening, Chloe was climbing the walls. She'd spent the day cooped up in Derek's house after he refused to let her go to the clinic with him. He'd ordered her to lay low, insisting she needed to stay out of sight in case Felix was watching her apartment or following her around town. She knew Derek was right, but after working at his busy clinic for three weeks, sitting idle for an entire day had been boring as hell.

She'd passed the time cleaning Derek's house from top to bottom, watching TV, taking a nap, leaving a message with her contact back in L.A. and then puttering around the kitchen for two hours cooking dinner. She figured having a warm meal on the table for Derek was the least she could do, a way to repay him for taking her in without a single complaint.

But she didn't expect the burst of joy she felt when he strode through the door. She was so genuinely happy to see him that it startled her. As did the flicker of desire that rippled through her when he fixed those deep brown eyes on her and his sensual mouth quirked in a smile.

"Hey," he said easily. He sniffed the air. "What smells so good?"

"Dinner." She awkwardly played with the hem of her blue angora sweater. "I commandeered your kitchen. I hope you don't mind."

"Mind? I'm tempted to throw myself at the floor and kiss your feet," he said with a grin. "I'm starving."

As he shrugged out of his long wool coat, Chloe's heart beat a little faster. His hunter-green long-sleeved shirt stretched over his broad shoulders and his black trousers emphasized his trim hips and taut ass. Her body's reaction to this man confused her. Heart pounding, palms tingling, breasts heavy. It was weird—she'd always been attracted to flashier men, men like Felix, with perfectly styled hair, sophisticated clothes, somewhat of a swagger.

Derek Colton, however, was not flashy in the slightest. He possessed an understated elegance. A simple sense of style, that no-nonsense buzz cut, a quiet astuteness and easygoing demeanor. He was confident but not arrogant. Gentle but no pushover.

And whenever she got within two feet of him, she wanted to kiss the living daylights out of him.

Brain out of the gutter, Chloe.

Swallowing, she banished the inappropriate thoughts and smiled tentatively. "Do you want to eat in the kitchen or the dining room?"

"Kitchen. The dining room feels too formal. Let me just wash my hands and I'll meet you there."

God, he washed his hands before dinner. Somehow that made her pulse race even faster. Derek Colton was a gentleman right down to the core.

When Derek walked in a few minutes later, Chloe had already set the table and was straining on her tiptoes, attempting to reach the wineglasses in the top cupboard. With a chuckle, Derek came up behind her and said, "Let me do that."

A shiver danced up her spine. Her hair was up in a ponytail, exposing the nape of her neck, and his hot breath fanned over her skin, making her giddy with desire. She inhaled sharply, only to breathe in the scent of his aftershave and another wave of giddiness crashed over her.

Trying to quell her rampant hormones, she darted toward the stove, keeping her back to him. If he knew how badly he affected her, he'd probably be horrified. Derek had never shown anything more than professional interest in her.

Oblivious to her thoughts, he carried the glasses to the table while Chloe served up the food.

His brown eyes widened when he saw everything she'd prepared—pot roast, garlic mashed potatoes, seasoned carrots. For dessert she'd even baked a chocolate cake, which sat on the counter in a glass cake dish.

"This looks amazing." His face shone with pleasure. "Thanks for cooking, Chloe."

His words startled her. Felix had never thanked her for a single thing. Ever.

"You're welcome."

Silence fell over the table as they dug into their food. Chloe kept shooting surreptitious looks at Derek, gauging his reaction to the meal. From the little contented noises he made and the way he devoured his first helping and then served himself a second, she knew she'd done well. Another rush of pleasure flooded her belly.

"Where did you learn to cook like this?" he asked as he reached for the bottle of red wine and poured them each a glass.

She shrugged. "I lived alone for a lot of years. I had to learn how to survive on something other than frozen dinners. Once I married Felix, I didn't do any cooking. I only started again during these past six months."

Derek furrowed his brows. "He didn't want you to cook?"

"No. We had a housekeeper for that," she said flatly. "I wasn't allowed to clean, either. Or do laundry. Anything domestic, really. He paid other people to do it, and he'd get angry if I tried to do anything myself."

She felt her cheeks go hot, knowing how pathetic she sounded, how weak for letting her husband forbid her to do basic tasks.

But Derek didn't react with distaste—he simply nodded in understanding. "He sounds very controlling."

"He is." She couldn't help but snort. "But Felix is nothing compared to his mother. That woman is a real piece of work. A controlling, overbearing, terrifying piece of work."

He raised a brow before sipping his wine. "I take it you weren't close to her."

"Uh, no. Bianca despised me," she told him. "From the second we met, she made it clear that she disapproved of me. She didn't think I was good enough for her precious son, but truthfully, I don't think *anyone* is good enough for Felix in her eyes. That woman made my life a living hell from day one."

"My mother-in-law wasn't much better," Derek confessed.

Chloe faltered, wanting to know more but afraid to ask. This was the first time he'd mentioned his marriage, and she didn't want to scare him off by asking too many questions. It was like walking on thin ice—one wrong move and the ice broke, taking any insight to this man with it.

"How long were you married?" she asked hesitantly.

His eyes grew shuttered. "Nine years." And just like that, he steered the conversation back to her. "So Felix didn't stand up to his mother when she treated you badly?"

"No. He worships the ground Bianca walks on." She shook her head. "Their relationship is a tad unsettling, if I'm being honest. They're very close—they tell each other everything, even private details, like, um, about sex and such. And she moved in with us about four years into the marriage, which was horrible."

"Was she ill or something?"

"Nope. She moved in to 'help me out.' And trust me, living under the same roof as that shrew was pure torture. She criticized everything I did. She bad-mouthed me to the housekeeper. She snooped in our bedroom." Chloe frowned. "She was convinced I was cheating on Felix and was determined to prove it."

"And your husband just let her get away with it?" Derek said in amazement.

"Like I said, Bianca can do no wrong in his eyes. I bet she threw a huge party when she heard I was dead. She couldn't wait to get rid of me."

Setting down his wineglass, Derek reached across the table for her hand.

Chloe jumped in surprise when his warm fingers encircled hers. His thumb stroked the center of her palm, sending a blast of lust that settled right between her legs.

"I'm sorry you had to go through all that," he said. "There are some really rotten people in this world, huh?"

"Yeah," she stammered, unable to think when he was touching her hand like that.

She stared at their intertwined fingers, the contrast of his darker skin with her pale skin. Then she lifted her head and met his eyes, stunned by the sudden flash of heat she saw there. What would his kiss feel like? Warm and gentle? Teasing? Rough and desperate? She wanted so badly to find out but knew she wouldn't. Couldn't, actually. She was in no position to start a relationship. Now that Felix knew she was alive, she would have to run again. Disappear. Leave Derek behind. It wouldn't be fair to him, to either one of them, if she started something up only to abandon him in the end.

Yet she couldn't break the eye contact, couldn't stop herself from imagining how it would feel to lean forward and kiss that sexy mouth of his, run her fingertips over his muscular chest, stroke that strong line of his jaw.

After a second, she cleared her throat, forcing herself to look away. "So…how about some dessert?"

"Thanks again for cooking," Derek remarked as he and Chloe stepped onto the porch a while later. He shot her a wry smile. "I think I'm getting spoiled. I can't remember the last time I cooked for myself. Always too busy."

Holding her steaming coffee mug, Chloe stood next to him, her hazel eyes focused on the rolling hills in the distance. They both wore their winter coats and gloves, and around her neck Chloe had looped a bright red scarf, which brought out the honey highlights of her hair and the flecks of green around her pupils. Her cheeks were flushed, and for the first time since he'd met her, she seemed genuinely relaxed.

"I don't know how you do it," she said softly.

"What, not cook?" he joked.

"No. How you do everything you do. Run your practice, oversee this ranch, raise Piper and Sawyer. Do you ever take time for yourself, Derek?"

Discomfort moved through him. He sank onto one of the wicker chairs on the porch and balanced his mug on his knee. After a moment, Chloe sat beside him.

"Well?" she prompted. "Do you?"

"Sometimes," he said vaguely.

"Yeah?" Her eyebrows lifted in challenge. "Name one thing you did recently that was only about you, only *for* you."

He mulled it over, then offered a smug smile. "I spent all of last Sunday on the couch, wearing sweats and watching football."

"Really?"

"Yep."

Her brows rose higher. "The *entire* day?"

"Well, I may have paid a quick visit to a patient between the afternoon and evening games."

"Did the patient call you?"

He avoided her eyes. "Yes…fine, no. But she's having a complicated pregnancy and I was worried."

She burst out laughing. "See? You're incapable of being selfish."

His stomach clenched. "That's not entirely true." He raised his mug to his lips and downed some coffee, hoping the distraction would stop him from saying anything more. But after he swallowed and lowered the mug, he couldn't control his next words from slipping out. "My wife accused me of being selfish on a daily basis."

Surprise flitted across Chloe's face. "I find that hard to believe."

"That she'd accuse me of that?"

"That she'd actually believe it to be true." A startling note of confidence filled her voice. "I've known you less than a month, yet it's easy to see that you live your life for other people, Derek. You're devoted to your patients, your family, your friends—even strangers, like me. If your wife truly thought you were selfish, then she didn't know you at all."

Her conviction floored him. So did the way she reached out to touch his knee in a reassuring squeeze. It was the first time Chloe had touched him willingly, without hesitation. And the moment she made contact, a rush of desire sizzled through his veins, dampening his palms and quickening his pulse.

Sitting this close to her, he could smell the sweet scent of her hair. His fingers tingled with the urge to stroke those blond strands. To pull her close and kiss her.

"How did your wife die?"

Chloe's soft-spoken inquiry snuffed out any feelings of desire. Before he could stop them, the memories spiraled to the surface, making his throat tighten.

The red-and-blue lights flashing on the bridge. The splintered wooden railing. The sleek back end of the SUV sticking out of the dark water, wheels up, rear windshield wipers still furiously working away.

The look in the sheriff's eyes when Derek approached.

The hot streak of agony when he'd peered over the edge of the bridge and witnessed the carnage below.

"Derek?"

Chloe's grip on his knee tightened. When he found the courage to meet her eyes, he saw nothing but sympathy and sweet understanding in those hazel depths.

"Car accident," he choked out, clutching his mug so tightly he feared the ceramic might shatter.

"Sawyer mentioned she died two years ago."

He frowned. When had Sawyer told Chloe that? And why the hell had they even been discussing Tess?

He quickly forced away the irritation. He didn't like it when people discussed his private life, but he couldn't fault Sawyer for it. The kid was only eleven years old, too young to realize just how devastated Derek still was about Tess's death.

"Yes. Two years," he confirmed.

"That must have been very hard for you, losing your wife." She hesitated. "Did you love her deeply?"

He nodded. "We were college sweethearts. Met at nineteen, married at twenty."

"Was she a doctor like you?"

"No, Tess majored in history. She wanted to be a teacher, and she had a job lined up in Philadelphia after we graduated. But then my folks died and we had to move to Eden Falls. There weren't any open teaching positions at the time, so she ended up staying home and taking care of Sawyer and Piper." Regret moved through him. "That's what she meant about me being selfish. I dumped my kid sister and brother on her while I built my medical career, forcing her into motherhood."

Chloe frowned. "She didn't want to be a mother?"

"She did, but not a year into our marriage. And not a mother to a six-month-old baby and a four-year-old who weren't even hers."

Her frown deepened. "Those two kids had just lost their parents. Please don't be offended, but I think that's incredibly selfish on *her* part. Piper and Sawyer might not have been bio-logically hers, but in a sense, she *was* their mother. They were only babies when your folks died. They needed you."

Emotion lined his throat. Chloe sounded so upset he leaned closer and wrapped one arm around her shoulder. She stiffened for a second, then sagged into the embrace.

"If Felix had brought two motherless babies into our home, I would have welcomed them with open arms," she murmured.

Yes, he imagined she would have. Her heart was bigger than this damn ranch, and she seemed to possess an innate need to soothe and nurture those around her. Not Tess, though; by the time she'd died, Tess had been too wrapped up in her own head to worry about the people around her.

"Your husband is a fool," he heard himself rasp.

Chloe's breath hitched. "What?"

"He is a fool," Derek repeated. "For not appreciating what he had. For not *seeing* what he had."

Pink splotches stained her cheeks, making her look young and unbelievably appealing. "How can you say that? You barely know me."

"I know that you're the best damn nurse I've ever worked with. I know that you're brave as hell."

Her face collapsed. "I was weak," she corrected in a wobbly voice.

Setting his mug on the little table between their chairs, Derek brought his hands to her face and cupped her cheeks. To his surprise, she leaned into his touch, rubbing her chin against his palm.

"You were strong," he said gruffly. "You placed yourself at Felix's mercy to protect your father. You got stuck in a situation beyond your control but you eventually found a way out of it."

"Some way out," she muttered as she put her own mug down. "I'm right back where I started, under Felix's thumb."

He remembered the bloodstained dress and his jaw tensed. "He won't hurt you again, Chloe. I'll make sure of it."

Desperation crept into her tone. "I can't stay at the ranch forever, Derek. I have to make some decisions. Figure out what to do now that he knows I'm alive."

She was going to run again.

Derek suddenly knew it with a certainty that went bone-deep. She'd agreed to stay with him until she decided her next move, but as he looked into her eyes, he realized she'd always known what that move would be.

His hands dropped from her face. "You're trying to get a new identity, aren't you?"

Guilt flickered in her gaze. "I placed a call to my contact this morning. He hasn't gotten back to me yet."

"So you're going to run for the rest of your life? Become different people and try to stay one step ahead of Felix?"

"What else can I do?" She looked as if she was grinding her teeth, her cheeks hollow, jaw taut. "Tell the cops that my husband beat me so I faked my death? I have no proof of the abuse—the case probably wouldn't even go to trial, and if it did, Felix would kill me before I could take the stand. I can file for divorce, but he'd still come after me eventually. Knowing him, he'd wait a couple of years, make me think I was safe, and then arrange for me to suffer an unfortunate accident."

She let out a breath. "He'll try to force me to come home, and when I refuse, he'll find a way to get rid of me. He won't be able to leave me alone, Derek. It'll eat him alive, knowing that I left him, that he couldn't control me, and so he'll come after me or my dad. Unless I hide, and do a better job of it this time."

"Chloe—"

"Maybe working as a nurse again was a bad idea," she cut in, sounding distressed. "I had enough money to disappear, to live on some island in the Caribbean and spend the rest of my days lying on the beach, but I wanted so badly to be useful again. To help people. Felix ordered me to give up nursing when we got married, and I was so eager to get back into it that I didn't think it through."

Anger bubbled in Derek's gut. Not directed at Chloe, but at her husband for placing her in this position. Making her yet again give up a career she so clearly loved.

"There has to be a better alternative," he said firmly. "You can't live the rest of your damn life in hiding, damn it."

A smile fluttered over her lips. "Two curse words in one sentence—you're really angry, aren't you?"

"Damn right I am." An uncharacteristic burst of rage jolted through him. "Your husband is a tyrant, sweetheart, and someone needs to clock him for the way he treated you. You're an amazing woman, Chloe. You deserve a helluva lot more than what that bastard—"

She kissed him.

Shock slammed into Derek's chest as her mouth met his, as her arms came up around his neck and pulled him close. Her lips were cold but the kiss was hotter than he'd ever anticipated. A fleeting brush of mouths, a seductive meeting of tongues. She tasted like coffee and chocolate frosting and something utterly feminine.

Pure desire swirled down his chest and tightened his groin, prompting him to slide his fingers inside her coat and grip her slender waist. Chloe made a whimpering sound as he took control, deepening the kiss, thrusting his tongue in her mouth to explore every sweet, hot crevice. Christ, her mouth felt so good against his. Her tongue eager, her hands even more so as she stroked the nape of his neck before digging her fingers into his shoulders and bringing him even closer.

He was two seconds from yanking her onto his lap and ripping that coat—and everything else—right off her, when his mind finally registered what his foolish mouth and hands were doing.

With a groan, he wrenched his lips free, breathing heavily, unable to meet her eyes.

Crap. What was he *doing?* He couldn't kiss this woman.

She kissed you.

The distinction didn't dim the panic rippling in his muscles. Playing who-kissed-who wouldn't make a lick of a difference. No matter how much he craved her, he couldn't get involved with her. Her marital status aside, he was in no frame of mind for a new relationship. Not now, and possibly not ever. The mere thought of opening himself up again, of giving his heart to someone else, turned his mouth to sawdust.

"Oh, God. I'm sorry, Derek."

Chloe's contrite voice gave him the courage to meet her eyes. She looked as startled and panicked as he felt, with guilt mingled in there, too.

"I shouldn't have done that," she added, her cheeks turning pink again. "I don't know what came over me."

He cleared his throat. Tried to erase the memory of how incredible she'd tasted, how soft and pliant her lips had felt against his. "It's okay."

"No, it's not," she said miserably. "I threw myself at you like a horny teenager, for Pete's sake."

Oh, man, did she have to use the word *horny?* Because that happened to be his current state of being, which he tried to hide by shifting on the chair and praying she didn't look down at his crotch. He hadn't been with a woman in two years and that one kiss had set his entire body on fire.

"I'm sorry," Chloe said again. "I didn't mean to take advantage of your hospitality. I know that me staying here doesn't mean that…well, that you and I are going to…you know."

He banished the stream of wicked images that her words inspired in his mind and forced a casual tone. "You don't have to apologize. And trust me, if anyone took advantage of anyone just now, it was me. I knew you were upset and not thinking clearly, yet I still—"

"I didn't kiss you because I was upset," she interrupted with a frazzled sigh.

He gulped. "No?"

"No." Her voice grew husky. "I kissed you because I've wanted to do that since the day we met."

Oh, hell. Did she have to look at him like that? With those heavy-lidded eyes and shy expression? It only made him want to kiss her again.

He drew a long breath. "We can't get involved, Chloe. For so many reasons."

"I know." She offered a rueful look. "First and foremost, I'm still married."

"And I'm still grieving," he said gruffly.

"We work together."

"Your life is in danger."

"So is yours, if Felix suspects we're together."

A short silence descended, and then Chloe laughed. "Any other reasons you can think of?"

Derek had to smile. "No, but I'm sure there are a few we're forgetting."

"But those are the important ones." She sounded sad.

"Yeah."

The next silence was tinged with regret, but Derek knew it was better to derail this train before it hurtled into dangerous territory and they both ended up getting hurt. Chloe must have agreed because she stood abruptly, reaching for their empty mugs.

"I think I'll head inside. It's getting chilly out here." As if to punctuate the remark, her breath left a white cloud in the night air.

Derek rose, too. "Yeah, it is getting cold."

They were two steps to the door when they heard footsteps crunching on the frost-covered grass. Derek turned to see his brother Tate clamoring up the front walk toward the porch.

An alarm immediately went off in his gut. Tate's expression was grave, hinting that this visit was more than a social call.

"Hey. I thought you were going back to Philly," Derek said with a frown.

"I'm heading out soon," Tate replied. "Just wanted to come by and give you this news in person." His blue-green eyes shifted to Chloe. "I'm not much for small talk, so I'll get right to the point."

She furrowed her brows. "Okay."

"I made some calls and I'm beginning to believe your suspicions might be warranted," Tate said grimly. "I think your husband knows you're alive."

Chapter 7

A shiver of fear snaked up Chloe's body and settled into a lump at the back of her throat. She swallowed hard, trying to quell the panic bubbling in her belly. Tate's news didn't surprise her, but she'd been hoping he'd come here to tell her she was overreacting. That Felix was in Malibu, busy with his surgeries and still mourning his beloved wife.

"Do you know for sure?" Derek asked sharply.

She noticed that Derek had taken a protective step toward her, but he didn't make a move to take her hand or put his arm around her. She didn't blame him. After the way she'd thrown herself at him only minutes ago, he was probably loath to touch her again.

She forced the memory of that impulsive kiss from her mind and focused on Tate.

"No, I'm not a hundred percent on this," Derek's brother answered. "You told me to be discreet, so I didn't want to raise any flags by asking too many questions. I spoke to Moreno's receptionist, who said the good surgeon is out of town. When I pushed for more details, she admitted that he's consulting on a case on the East Coast, but that he's scheduled to return to L.A. sometime next week."

"East Coast," Chloe echoed flatly.

She suddenly felt light-headed. A part of her had prayed that she was wrong and Felix wasn't the one sending her those wedding souvenirs, that maybe someone was playing a sick joke on her. But who was she kidding? Nobody else she knew was twisted enough to mess with her head like this. Felix, however, excelled at psychological manipulation. He knew how to find a person's weakness and exploit it, how to tease and torment until he drove someone utterly insane.

"I also got a call from the lab," Tate added. He glanced at Chloe. "You were right about the blood—it wasn't human."

She frowned. "What was it, then?"

"Pig's blood. And there's no way to trace where it came from. Most butchers have pig's blood on hand, so it's easy to get. Some grocery stores even sell it in the fresh meat section."

"We don't need to trace it," Chloe mumbled. "Felix is the one who left me the dress."

"I know you don't want to hear this," Tate said, "but I think you need to involve the police. I can drive you down to the precinct in Philly myself and help you file a restraining order."

She offered a weak laugh. "A restraining order won't stop him."

"Chloe—" Derek started.

"Thank you for looking into this," she interrupted, turning to Tate. "I'll let you know what I decide to do."

Without letting either man respond, she darted into the house.

Her heart thudded in an irregular rhythm as she hurried toward the guest bedroom, her legs so shaky she could barely stay upright. When she burst into the room, the fear and desperation swirling inside her transformed into a gust of fury, a blast of frustration, a rush of resentment.

Damn him.

Damn him.

Chloe curled her hands into fists, resisting the urge to pick up the lamp on the bedside table and hurl it into the wall.

She'd finally been *free.* She'd *escaped,* damn it!

Over the past six months, she'd actually seen a gleam of

hope in her future. She was doing the work she'd loved before Felix forced her to quit. She'd felt a sense of peace knowing her father was safe, certain that Felix wouldn't be bothered by one old man now that he didn't need leverage to keep Chloe in line. She'd even found a hometown, a place where she felt needed, liked and respected.

And now Felix had crushed all that hope, the way he crushed everything else in her life. Her self-esteem, her femininity, her peace of mind.

A soft knock sounded on the door. "Chloe?" Derek called. "Can I come in?"

She opened her mouth to say yes, then halted, realizing what a mistake that would be. She couldn't keep leaning on this man. Couldn't take advantage of his strength and generosity. He was giving her a place to stay, and that was already too much. An involvement between the two of them would lead to nothing but disaster, especially with Felix hanging over her head like a black cloud.

"Chloe?"

She took a shaky breath and said, "Derek, I'd like to be alone for a bit, if you don't mind."

After a beat, he responded. "All right."

Once his footsteps retreated, Chloe sank on the edge of the mattress and buried her head in her hands. Tears stung her eyes, but she blinked them away, refusing to succumb to the urge to bawl like a baby.

She couldn't hide at Derek's ranch forever. She knew that. But for the life of her, she didn't know what to do anymore. She'd already faked her death and moved to the other side of the country, and Felix had still found her. So what now?

Squaring her shoulders, she stood up and walked over to the dresser where she'd left her cell phone. She checked the screen, but there were no missed calls or messages. Her friend from L.A. hadn't gotten back to her yet, which meant she couldn't make any moves yet. Once she got the ball rolling on her new identity, she could formulate a solid plan. Maybe she'd go to Australia—there were lots of places to hide down under. Or Europe—it was easy to disappear in a big city or somewhere in the countryside, perhaps.

All of those options, however, brought an ache to her heart. No matter where she went, she'd have to leave Derek behind, and the thought of that was surprisingly gloomy. In a mere month, Derek had managed to get under her skin.

Her body began to tingle, her mouth going dry as she relived that one thrilling kiss, the sheer sense of belonging that enveloped her when her lips had met Derek's.

Belonging. But no, she *didn't* belong. Not in Eden Falls. Not in Derek's life. And certainly not in Derek's bed.

Felix had made certain of that.

Tate Colton had just finished packing his duffel bag when his cell phone rang. A glance at the display revealed Hugo Villanueva's number. Finally.

"Are we all set?" Tate said in lieu of greeting.

His supervisor chuckled. "Tired of spinning your wheels, Colton?"

"Hell, yes. I'm ready to nail these bastards."

"Good because your documents just landed on my desk and we've got the green light to go ahead with the op. I need you in Philly so I can brief you on your cover and objectives."

Satisfaction flooded Tate's gut. "I'm packing as we speak. I'll probably get in late tonight, but I can be at your office first thing tomorrow morning."

"Good. I'll see you then."

Tate hung up and bent down to zip his duffel, then crossed the spacious bedroom. His case files sat on the splintered pine desk he'd used since he was a child. His parents hadn't redecorated any of their children's bedrooms once Tate, Derek, Gunnar and Emma had left the nest, and he always experienced a sense of peace and familiarity when he came home. Everything in the bedroom reminded him of his folks—the custom desk his father had built for him, the dark green curtains his mom had sewn herself, the old posters and family photographs hanging on the cream-colored walls.

Although he'd been living in Philly ever since he'd made detective, this ranch was home and always would be.

As he picked up the blue file folders, one of them flew open, its contents fluttering onto the hardwood floor.

Suppressing a sigh, Tate knelt to scoop up the strewn papers. He shoved the witness statements, case notes and photos back into the folder, but froze when his fingers collided with one photograph in particular.

After the visceral reaction he'd experienced the first time he'd seen it, he'd been making a conscious effort to avoid looking at this one image. As a detective, he needed to stay objective, to separate himself from the victims and look at the facts, but when it came to Hannah Troyer, he seemed to operate on emotion rather than objectivity.

Now, as he gazed at those big blue-gray eyes and delicate, doll-like features, that same hot rush of emotion returned, making his throat go tight. Hannah had been missing for more than a month now and the only clue to her disappearance had been the anonymous video that had surfaced on the internet, featuring a clearly drugged Hannah mouthing what looked like "help me."

Watching that had ripped Hannah's brother Caleb apart, and although Tate had tried to remain professional, the video had nearly killed him, too. Seeing that beautiful redhead on the screen pleading for help had left him paralyzed with pure helplessness.

"We'll find her."

Tate jumped, startled to find his sister Emma looming over him. He hadn't even heard her enter the room—that's how focused he'd been on Hannah Troyer's lovely face.

"I know," he said brusquely.

But will she be alive?

Neither said it out loud, but Tate knew they were both thinking it. His heart twisted once more as the terrifying scenario flashed through his mind. Hannah. Dead.

"How's Caleb doing?" he asked, trying not to dwell on the unthinkable.

"Good, considering." Emma's green eyes softened. "He's spending a lot of time with his girls. He's scared to let them out of his sight."

"I don't blame him." In fact, Tate hoped the rest of the Amish folk kept a closer eye on their children. After Mary Yoder's kidnapping and Violet Chastain's attack, it had become clear that nobody was safe in Paradise Ridge and wouldn't be until this depraved sex ring was out of commission.

"And you?" Tate pushed. "How are you doing, tomato-head?"

His use of her childhood nickname made her scowl. "I'm fine. Great, actually." Her scowl faded into a secretive smile, and he knew she must be thinking about Caleb.

"Still determined to give up your modern perks for a more traditional way of life?"

She nodded slowly. "Yeah, I think I am."

He was about to tease her about the hell of living without a blow dryer and cell phone but quickly stopped himself. Emma's imminent conversion to the Amish church was important to her and she already got enough ribbing about it from Gunnar and Piper. Besides, who was Tate to judge? What did he really have going for him in his own life, aside from an empty apartment in Philly and a badge that didn't seem to be helping him find those missing girls?

So he simply nodded in return and said, "I hope you get everything you want out of it, Em."

She looked surprised but touched. "Thanks, Tate." Her green eyes drifted back to the photograph he still gripped in his hand. "We're going to find her," she said again.

Tate swallowed. "Yes, we will."

* * *

"I don't like this," Derek said for the tenth time in ten minutes. His profile revealed a stiff jaw and tight lips, a clear sign that—as he kept insisting—he really, really didn't like this.

But Chloe held her ground as he steered the car to the small lot at the back of the clinic. "It'll be fine," she assured him. "You'll be with me the whole time."

"I'd feel better if you were at my house, behind locked doors and a security alarm," he grumbled.

"I did that yesterday, and I almost went crazy from inactivity. I need to work," she said firmly. "I need to feel useful."

"You also need to stay safe."

"I'll be safe here with you," she insisted. She stuck out her chin. "Quit arguing with me, Colton. I'm working today and you can't stop me."

"I could fire you…"

"You wouldn't." She smiled smugly. "I'm too much of an asset."

He shot her a sidelong look, his lips quirking. "Are you always so stubborn? And arrogant?"

She had to laugh. "Stubborn, yes. Arrogant, no."

His answering laugh made her heart skip a beat. She took a deep breath, trying to steady her pulse and remind herself that she couldn't let this man affect her, at least not on a romantic level. Doctor and nurse. One friend helping out another. That was all they could be to each other from this point on.

They entered the building from the rear door, going their separate ways in the fluorescent-lit hallway. Chloe changed into her scrubs and tied her hair in a ponytail, then wandered out to the reception area to greet Derek's receptionist, who offered her a tall foam cup of coffee.

"Thanks, Nancy," she said gratefully.

For the next several hours, Chloe helped Derek tend to their patients, dealing with everything from minor issues like refilling prescriptions to major ones like stitching up the gaping cut the diner's chef had incurred while chopping onions.

By the time four o'clock rolled around, Chloe had completely forgotten about Felix. Derek's practice was too busy, offering no opportunities to dwell on her own messed-up problems.

As usual, Sawyer showed up after school let out, trailed by Piper, who smiled at Chloe as the duo approached Nancy's desk. "Hi, Amelia," Piper said.

"Hi, Piper," she said warmly. "You're going to help out in the clinic today?"

The blonde shook her head in irritation. "Nope. I'm supposed to drive the twerp home, but he insisted on coming here first to finish up his 'filing.'"

"I promised Derek I would," Sawyer said in a firm voice.

Chloe grinned as the boy darted down the hall. Although Derek sometimes let Sawyer into the exam rooms—after making sure the patient didn't mind—he usually assigned his brother random tasks around the clinic, trivial little things that Sawyer treated as utterly important and tackled with enthusiasm.

"I'll be in the waiting room," Piper said, sighing. She pulled her iPod and earbuds from her canvas shoulder bag as she wandered off.

Chloe called in their last patient of the day, and once the appointment ended, she headed for the back office to change into her street clothes. She'd just zipped up her leather boots when Sawyer appeared in the doorway, a thoughtful look on his face.

"I figured it out," he announced.

She gave him a quizzical look. "Figured what out?"

"Why you don't like kids."

An arrow of grief sliced into her heart. Oh, God. She should've known the boy had noticed the way she kept her distance from him, but knowing that it had bothered him enough to give it serious thought brought the sting of tears to her eyes. Her inability to get close to Sawyer had nothing to do with the boy and everything to do with her, but she knew he would never understand that. It tore her apart, his thinking she hated children.

"Sawyer," she began thickly.

"No, it's okay. Listen, I think you don't like kids because you're just not used to them. Am I right?"

She couldn't answer—the lump in her throat was that big.

"I think I'm right," he went on with a nod. "A lot of people aren't used to kids. They don't know how to talk to them."

Her eyes stung. Her throat grew even tighter.

"They don't know if they should talk to us like we're children or grown-ups or whatever." Sawyer flashed her an endearing smile. "But you've just gotta talk to us the way you talk to anyone else."

Her heart cracked in two. Sawyer Colton was…he was simply something else. The sweetest kid she'd ever met. Wiser than most of the adults she knew, and so adorable it took all of her willpower to control the tears threatening to spill over.

"I think you'd like kids if you spent more time with them," he finished. "If you want, we can hang out a lot so you'll get used to it."

Chloe blinked rapidly, sucking oxygen into her burning lungs. When she got her emotions under control, she met his brown eyes. "Thank you, Sawyer. That's a really sweet offer."

"Maybe I'll come over tomorrow and we can play cards," he suggested. "Derek's teaching me how to play poker. Do you know how to play?"

She nodded weakly.

"Good, so you can give me some tips, too. Later, Amelia."

With a little wave, he bounded off, leaving her staring after him in shock and dismay.

Derek ducked into his office as Sawyer came barreling down the hall. He didn't want his brother to know he'd been eavesdropping, especially since he'd reprimanded Sawyer for doing the same thing countless times before. But Derek hadn't been able to resist when he'd heard Chloe's and Sawyer's voices drifting out of the back office.

I think you don't like kids because you're just not used to them.

Man, that kid was something else. Derek experienced a rush of pride when he realized that he could take at least partial credit for the perceptive, caring kid Sawyer had grown up to be. Derek and his siblings had raised Sawyer, tried to instill the same values their adoptive parents had drilled into them, and clearly their efforts hadn't been futile.

"We're leaving! See you at home, bro!" Piper's voice wafted from the front room.

Derek called out a goodbye, then stepped into the hall and headed for the office Chloe and Sawyer had been chatting in. When he noticed that the door was shut, he frowned. The frown deepened when a soft noise perked his ears. Was that… sobbing?

Wary, he placed his ear to the door. Silence…and then a tiny whimper. Choked breaths. Another sob.

Without bothering to knock, he threw the door open.

And found Chloe sitting against the wall with her arms wrapped around her knees, crying as if her heart was breaking.

Her head lifted at his entrance and as their eyes locked, she released an unstable breath and whispered, "I don't hate kids."

He was at her side in a nanosecond, down on the floor, pulling her right into his arms. She rested her head on his chest and cried, her delicate shoulders shuddering from each hoarse breath, each tormented whimper. He stroked the small of her back, murmuring words of comfort, holding her tight, running his fingers through her silky hair. After several long minutes, her body stopped trembling. Her sobs faded.

She looked up at him, her eyes red and puffy, her cheeks wet from her tears. "I had four babies," she whispered.

Shock coursed through him. "What?"

"Four babies. And they all died." Agony hung from her words. "They all died, Derek."

Her revelation caused his heart to fracture in a few more places. Suddenly it all made sense—her determination to keep Sawyer at a distance, the way she smiled politely but without her usual warmth around younger patients. How stricken she'd looked when she'd seen Violet's toddlers the night she'd come to the ranch for dinner.

"Do you…" He cleared his throat. "Do you want to talk about it, sweetheart?"

"I guess I should, huh?"

"Only if you want to," he said gruffly. "I would never force you to confide in me."

"I know." She wiped her cheeks with her sleeve, then wiggled out of his embrace. "Will you give me a second to collect myself?"

Nodding, he stood up, helping her to her feet. "I'll send Nancy home and meet you in my office," he said.

Before he left the room, he saw Chloe reach into her purse for a pack of tissues. He heard her blowing her nose as he strode to the lobby, and his heart continued to ache, a dull throbbing that made it difficult to breathe. He spoke to Nancy, who was already getting ready to leave. After she left, he locked the door of the clinic and hurried to his office.

A part of him wasn't sure he wanted to know Chloe's story. It hit too close to home, summoned unwanted memories to the surface, memories that already haunted his nightmares. But his curiosity beat out the apprehension, and his strides were quick as he entered the office.

Chloe sat in one of the visitor's chairs, and rather than walk around to his desk, Derek sank into the plush chair next to hers and reached for her hand. Her skin was cold, prompting him to cover her hand with both of his, trying to warm her up. Although her eyes were still rimmed with red, she'd touched up her makeup, and her face looked smooth and soft to the touch.

"Remember I mentioned those issues I had during my marriage?" she finally began, those hazel eyes locking with his.

He nodded.

"They were fertility issues. Or infertility, I guess." Her bitterness was unmistakable. "Felix and I really wanted kids, and we started trying a couple of years into the marriage. But nothing happened. We went to a fertility doctor and had tests done, but both of us were perfectly healthy. The doctor said to give it time, so we kept trying. After two more years, we finally gave up. Felix wasn't happy about it, but he had no interest in adoption or any other alternative methods, so we both resigned ourselves to not having children." She smiled faintly. "A week after we decided to give up, I got pregnant."

"That happens a lot," Derek admitted. "Sometimes there's no explanation for it, but it's almost like you're trying so hard to make it happen that you're, I don't know, jinxing it. And then you stop trying and *presto*."

"We were over the moon. Married for four years at that point, and we couldn't wait to start a family." Her expression grew sad. "I miscarried after four months. We were disappointed, but I was still young and there was no reason not to try again. Six months later, I got pregnant again. This time I lasted five months before the miscarriage."

Derek squeezed her hand. "I'm so sorry, Chloe."

"So was I." She shook her head in anger. "Felix didn't take the second miscarriage too well. That's when he started with the subtle putdowns. He said I must have done something wrong, blamed me for losing the baby. By that time, his mother had moved in with us to help with the baby, and like I said, Bianca is an absolute monster. She drove me nuts during the entire pregnancy, and sometimes I wonder if all the stress she caused me might have played a part in the miscarriage."

"Stress can definitely affect a pregnancy," Derek concurred.

"We waited two years before trying again, and the third pregnancy I actually carried to full term. We did genetic testing, and the doctor said everything looked perfectly fine." Her face collapsed, and her hand trembled beneath his. "It was a boy. Stillborn."

Derek's throat clogged. "God, sweetheart. That must have been devastating."

"It was. And Felix, he was furious. He started calling me defective and said I was depriving him of the one thing he wanted." She bit her bottom lip. "I was such a mess, Derek. I was desperate to please him, so I agreed to try for another baby. I thought if I gave him what he wanted, he would stop hitting me, stop taunting me. So, I got pregnant for the fourth and last time."

Derek's brows knit in a frown. "Did he stop the physical abuse during this last pregnancy?"

"No."

Anger whipped up his spine. "He still hit you, while you were carrying his child?"

She nodded numbly. "We did more testing to make sure the baby was okay, and supposedly he was, but I lost him, too, after two months. And I made it clear that I was not putting myself through that again. I refused to get pregnant ever again. By then, Felix had grown tired of being disappointed, so he agreed. But he didn't stop terrorizing me. If anything, he just got worse."

"And that's when you started seeing the therapist?"

"Yes, and, well, you know the rest of the story. I spent twelve years living with a maniac. *Twelve* years." She laughed without a shred of humor. "How weak does that make me, Derek?"

She hurried on before he could respond to that. "I don't hate Sawyer," she said softly. "If anything, I adore that kid. But it's hard for me to open my heart to him. He's exactly how I imagine my own boys would've turned out to be. They were all boys, all four babies I lost."

She continued chewing on her lower lip until Derek reached out and cupped her jaw, stilling her nervous nibbling. He dragged his thumb over her lips, unable to resist. Her mouth was so lush, so soft. Everything about her was soft—her skin, her hair, her curvy body. But not her will. Oh, no, this woman had nerves of steel. Despite the depression she'd struggled with and the abusive situation she'd found herself in, Chloe Moreno was not weak, no matter what she believed.

"You're not weak," he said softly. "You did the best you could in a screwed-up situation. You know how brave you were for trying to get pregnant after each miscarriage? Allowing yourself to hope despite the disappointment that kept preceding it?"

He traced the seam of her lips and heard her breath hitch. "And trust me, sweetheart, you are *not* defective. There could be any number of reasons why you miscarried, and that last miscarriage? I think your sadistic son of a bitch husband *beating* you during the pregnancy contributed to that outcome."

A fresh dose of anger shot through him like a cannonball as the image of Felix raising a hand to a pregnant Chloe flashed across his brain. What kind of man did that to the woman he claimed to love? And then to make her believe the loss of the baby was *her* fault, her *defect*?

His heart clenched, weeping for the woman sitting beside him. He suddenly became consumed with the need to show her how astounding she was, to prove just how *wanted* she was.

Before he could stop himself, he drew her into his arms, ignored her startled squeak and covered her mouth with his.

Chapter 8

Derek was kissing her. Chloe couldn't wrap her head around it, and as his skillful tongue teased her lips open, she decided to quit trying to figure it out. The kiss was electric. It made her skin buzz and her breasts tingle, sending pulses of heat down to her core.

Her eyes closed as Derek devoured her with his mouth. Her surroundings faded, her mind unable to register anything but the feel of those firm, warm lips teasing her into oblivion. She yelped when she felt herself being yanked to her feet, and the next thing she knew, her butt collided with a hard surface. Derek's desk.

Spreading her legs with his hands, Derek stepped into the cradle of her thighs and ground his lower body into hers, summoning a desperate moan from her lips. The hard ridge of his arousal pressing into her mound unleashed a storm of sexual excitement. Her nipples puckered and strained against the lace fabric of her bra. Her thighs clenched with need. Another moan slipped out.

Derek didn't break the kiss, not even when his hands began a slow, torturous exploration that made her breathless. When he squeezed her breasts over her shirt, Chloe shuddered with pleasure. When he dipped one hand beneath the waistband of her pants, she nearly fell right off the desk.

"Derek," she whimpered.

The fingers of his other hand dug into her hip, steadying her. Wrenching his mouth off hers, he met her eyes. "I've got you," he said gruffly. "I've got you, Chloe."

She didn't object when he slipped his hand under her bikini panties, palming her damp folds.

They released simultaneous groans.

The passion shining in his brown eyes stole the breath from her lungs. When he stroked her aching core and discovered the proof of her excitement, pure male satisfaction flashed across his handsome face. "You want this," he rasped.

"I *need* this," she choked out.

Sensing her desperation, Derek pressed his palm over her swollen sex, applying pressure to her clit with the heel of his hand. Pleasure skyrocketed through her.

"More," she begged.

Breathing hard, he increased his pace, the friction of his palm making her mindless with lust. When she felt the first ripples of release dancing in her belly, she wrapped her arms around his neck and yanked his head down for another kiss.

She exploded the moment their tongues met.

Crying out, Chloe dug her fingernails into his shoulders and gave herself over to the orgasm. Waves of bliss washed over her, heating her core, zipping over her fevered flesh, causing her mind to soar to a place where nothing but ecstasy and Derek existed.

When she finally crashed back to Earth, she let out a soft sigh, her lips curving in a sheepish smile. "Wow. That was unexpected."

Swallowing, Derek slowly removed his hand from her pants. Her gaze landed on the unmistakable bulge straining beneath his trousers, and her mouth watered, the need to touch him so strong she almost keeled over again.

Smiling, she glided her hand down his chest toward the tantalizing proof of his need.

His breathing grew labored. "I...we can't do this."

Chloe's smile faded when she noticed Derek's agonized expression.

That one disheartening look was all it took to kick-start her mental faculties. As common sense returned, she suddenly wanted to kick herself. So much for keeping her distance. Ten minutes alone with Derek and she'd succumbed to temptation like a lovesick teenager.

No matter how hard she tried, her brain turned to mush around this man. He was so different from Felix. He treated her with respect. He listened to her. He was the kind of man she'd fantasized about marrying when she was growing up, and now that the fantasy had become a reality, now that this perfect, wonderful man was right in front of her, she couldn't help but want to keep him close.

This had to stop, though. She couldn't keep kissing Derek Colton whenever it struck her fancy.

Why not?

The internal question gave her pause.

Why *not* see this through? She couldn't leave town until she secured a new identity, anyway. She was already staying at Derek's house. And the chemistry between them was clearly off the charts.

So why shouldn't she give in? Discover what being with an honorable man, a *good* man, could be like. She'd spent years trying to please her parents, then her patients, then her husband, and for the first time in her life, she wanted to please *herself.* To be selfish.

But it was obvious that Derek wasn't on the same page. From the way he kept dragging his hands over his scalp in frustration, she knew he intended on fighting the attraction to the bitter end.

"Hey, it's okay," she said in the midst of his evident despair.

"No, it's not." Torment swam in his brown eyes. "I want you, Chloe."

She blinked in surprise. "What?"

"I want you." His voice was hoarse. "I'm attracted to you, and I don't frickin' know what to do about it."

His honesty floored her. But why was she surprised? Derek was the most up-front man she'd ever met.

"I was just thinking the same thing," she admitted. "Wondering what to do about us."

"What'd you come up with?" he asked wryly.

She took a courageous breath, then exhaled in a rush. "That I want to be selfish. That I want to forget about everything and just be with you for as long as I can."

He shifted uneasily.

Chloe slid off the desk and took a step toward him. She thought he'd object, but when she placed her hand on the center of his muscular chest, he sagged into her touch.

"What's really going on, Derek?" she asked softly. "I know we talked about the reasons why getting involved would be a bad idea, but this goes deeper, doesn't it?" She studied his face. "Do you feel it'll be a betrayal to your wife if you got involved with me?"

He shook his head.

"Then what is it?"

The resulting silence brought the ache of disappointment, but just when she thought he wouldn't answer, he opened his mouth and shocked the hell out of her.

"If we got involved, I fear I'll end up disappointing you."

She gaped at him. "Why would you ever think that? God, Derek, you could never disappoint me. If anything, you're too good for me."

Sighing, Derek brought one hand to her face and gently stroked her cheek. Her left cheek. And it startled Chloe to realize she hadn't even flinched.

"Don't say things like that," he said roughly. "You're an incredible woman, Chloe. Any man would be lucky to have you."

He took her hand and moved it right over his heart. She felt the erratic beating vibrating beneath her fingertips. "But me?" he went on. "I'm not the big catch you think I am."

She highly doubted that. Derek was the kindest, most honorable man she'd ever met, and nothing he said would make her believe otherwise.

Sighing, she twined her fingers through his and led him back to the chairs, tugging on his arm to force him to sit next to her. "What happened to make you think that, Derek?" And why did she get the feeling it had everything to do with his late wife?

Sure enough, her suspicions proved correct.

"Tess happened." His deep voice cracked. "I couldn't save her. I couldn't heal her."

Her brows furrowed. "Was she sick?"

After a long beat, he nodded. "She was bipolar. I knew that before we got married—she told me when we first started dating. She was taking medication for it at that point and had the symptoms under control."

"But she went off the meds," Chloe guessed.

"Around the time we moved to Eden Falls. She said the meds made her feel as if she were living in a dream, like she wasn't herself." He made a frustrated grumble at the back of his throat. "She insisted that she could control the mood swings, and she was seeing a therapist, which seemed to help her. She'd be good for months at a time, and then suddenly she'd have a manic episode that lasted for days. Losing her temper, drinking, being hyperactive. She'd talk a mile a minute, freak out without provocation—she was just…well, manic."

Chloe squeezed his hand. From what she knew of the disorder, the manic periods often went hand in hand with depression, and so she said, "And then the depression would set in?"

His Adam's apple twitched as he gulped. "Big-time. She wouldn't eat, couldn't sleep. She threatened suicide every other minute, drank more. She would call me at the hospital—this was before I opened the clinic—and I'd rush home, expecting to find her dead."

His anguish dug deep creases in his face. "I begged her to go back on the meds, which she eventually agreed to do." His jaw clenched. "But she didn't take them regularly, and she kept messing around with the dosages, until I had to stand there every morning and make sure she took her pill. Then I'd take the whole bottle with me so she couldn't abuse it. Which only led her to consume more alcohol instead. It got to the point where I couldn't leave Sawyer or Piper with her anymore. That's why I hired Julia. I didn't trust Tess with them."

Chloe realized how difficult that must have been for him to admit. She lifted her hand and stroked the strong edge of his jaw, her heart breaking for him. It was funny, but she'd always imagined Derek's life to be perfect—adopted by wonderful parents, surrounded by loving siblings, successful in his career. It just went to show that you had no idea what went on behind closed doors.

"Julia agreed to work full-time, and Tess and I moved out of the big house," he went on. He clutched her hand, squeezing hard. "I did everything I could to help her, Chloe. I tried to be a good husband, a good provider. A shoulder for her to lean on, a support system. But nothing I did worked. She got worse, and the night before she—" He seemed to choke on the words. "The night before she died, I suggested we admit her to a psychiatric facility."

Chloe gasped. "I imagine she didn't take that well."

"Not at all, but I was at the end of my rope. I didn't know what to do." A tortured look entered his brown eyes. "She cried. Yelled. Hit me. Threw things. But in the end, she finally agreed that it might be for the best, that intense therapy combined with stronger medication might be the only solution." He paused, breathing hard. "She never made it to the facility. I'd opened the clinic by then and had to make a late house call to one of the Amish families in Paradise Ridge. Tess was sleeping when I left."

Dread climbed up Chloe's throat. "What happened?"

"I guess she started drinking when I was gone." His breathing grew shallow. "She phoned while I was with my patient, but I didn't take the call. She left a message, which I checked about an hour later. She sounded drunk, frantic. She said she needed air and was going for a drive."

"Oh, God," Chloe whispered.

"She mentioned Eden Falls Bridge in the message—it was one of her favorite places in town because it's right near the waterfall." Derek's voice took on a faraway note. "I drove there as fast as I could, but I was too late. When I pulled up to the bridge, the cops were already there, and our SUV was already in the river." He blew out a ragged breath. "Tess died on impact."

Without thinking twice, Chloe wrapped her arms around Derek's neck and pulled him close. She stroked his back in soothing motions, then tilted her head to meet his eyes. "Was it an accident, or…?" She let the question hang.

"I don't know," he croaked. He curled his hands into fists and rested them on Chloe's shoulders, his head dipping down in defeat. "To this day, I have no idea if she killed herself, or if the drinks she'd consumed that night caused her to lose control of the car. She didn't mention suicide in the message or leave a note, so I don't know, Chloe. I just don't know."

She held him tighter, cupping the back of his head and running her fingers over the bristly dark hairs of his buzz cut. "It's okay," she murmured.

"There's something else I didn't tell you." He gazed at her with wild eyes. "Tess was pregnant."

Chloe's jaw fell open.

"She never told me," Derek added, an uncharacteristic flash of anger glittering in his eyes. "The medical examiner said she was seventeen weeks along. It was a boy."

A sense of deep understanding passed between them when their gazes locked again. Chloe was stunned. She'd never dreamed that Derek might have lost a child, too. A boy. God, just like her boys, who she'd loved so desperately without having ever seen them.

"I know how devastating that must have been, losing not only your wife, but also your child," she whispered.

Derek let out a heavy breath. "I lie awake some nights, thinking about my son. About Tess. I haven't dated since they died. Haven't even thought about it." He laughed harshly. "The morning of her funeral, I decided I'd never open myself up to a relationship again."

Her own chuckle was equally bitter. "Yeah, I made that same vow the day I left Felix."

They looked at each other and smiled.

"Wow," Derek said mildly. "We're a real pair, huh?"

"We sure are."

Silence stretched between them. She still had her arms around him, his hands still rested on her shoulders. Their foreheads were nearly touching, their lips mere inches apart, but the air no longer sizzled with passion. It was now thick with tension and regret.

And before Derek even opened his mouth, Chloe knew what he would say.

"I'm not ready."

She swallowed her disappointment. "I know."

"That doesn't mean we can't be friends, though."

A laugh popped out of her mouth. "Friends," she echoed.

Derek nodded, his expression so earnest she didn't have the heart to object.

With another firm nod, he stood up, averting his eyes as he headed for the door. "Come on, let's lock up. We can pick up some takeout on the way home."

Utterly perplexed, Chloe watched him leave the office, wishing she could figure out what was going through his head right now—and knowing that no matter what Derek said, there was no way in hell the two of them could pretend this entire encounter hadn't happened and just be *friends*.

When the call finally came through on his cell phone, Felix Moreno was more than ready for it.

He'd been stuck in this damn hotel suite for the past few days, forced to twiddle his thumbs while he waited for the phone to ring. Not only that, but the patient he was scheduled to operate on had developed a secondary infection, so the surgery had been postponed until tomorrow. Felix loathed sitting idle, and the longer he remained in Philadelphia, the more he disliked the place.

"Has the package been delivered?" he barked into the phone.

"Not yet," a timid male voice replied. "It's en route as we speak."

Felix's grip tightened over the stem of his wineglass. The Cabernet swished, nearly spilling over the rim of the glass. Not one to waste expensive wine, Felix leaned forward and set the glass on the coffee table, his angry gaze fixing on the electric fireplace.

"En route," he echoed, his voice lined with displeasure. "It was supposed to be here already."

"I know, Dr. Moreno, but there were some minor hiccups."

"I don't have time for hiccups, minor or otherwise. I'm a busy man and my presence is required in Los Angeles. I can't stay in this godforsaken city indefinitely."

"You won't have to. Everything is on schedule now. I'll be in touch in a couple of days with the details." A pause. "Will your surgery be done by then?"

"It should be."

"I'll be in touch," the caller said again.

Felix disconnected and tossed the cell phone on the cushion next to him. Frowning, he picked up his wineglass and took a slow sip, but not even the familiar flavor of the heady vintage could erase his annoyance.

He was tired of this crap. His mother was growing more and more upset with him the longer he stayed away, and he truly hated displeasing Bianca. His receptionist's phone was ringing off the hook with patients and colleagues requesting Felix's services.

He rose from the sofa, angrily stalking to the window, where he once again studied the streets down below. He wanted nothing more than to say good riddance to this city and be on his way. But he couldn't do that.

Not until he took care of the bitch.

It didn't take a genius to figure out that Derek had shut down on her. After yesterday's confession in his office, the doctor was now going out of his way to avoid any conversations that bordered on personal, and Chloe was beginning to grow frustrated. During dinner last night, they'd discussed politics. Over breakfast this morning, the problems with the health care system. At the clinic, they spoke about patients. And now they were driving back to the ranch, and Derek was chatting about cereal. *Cereal,* of all things.

She understood, though. It must have been difficult for him to give her a glimpse into the suffering that hovered beneath that perfect exterior of his, and she suspected it embarrassed him to admit to those feelings of failure.

Why couldn't he see that the peek into his soul had only made him more appealing to her? His past made him more… *real.* If anything, it reinforced the sense of connection she felt toward him, and she wished he didn't view his past as a weakness but as something that had made him even stronger.

"I can't keep Lucky Charms in the house anymore," Derek was saying. "Sawyer picks out all the marshmallows, puts them in a bowl and dumps in the milk. A couple of years ago, the kid had eleven cavities when I took him to the dentist."

Chloe smiled. "He lives by his own rules, huh?"

"Damn straight." His voice rang with humor.

He steered onto the turnoff leading to the ranch, then slowed the car when they noticed a FedEx truck idling near the gate. Derek pulled alongside the truck just as the deliveryman hopped out with a small cardboard box tucked under his arm.

"Wait here. I'll save this guy a trip," Derek said, reaching for the door handle.

As the lanky, dark-haired FedEx guy headed for the intercom box mounted on the gate, Derek hopped out of the car to intercept him.

Chloe watched through the windshield, unconcerned—that is, until she saw Derek's broad shoulders stiffen. He peered at the package like it was a ticking time bomb, his jaw tighter than a drum as he signed for the delivery.

Her pulse drummed out a deafening beat, drowning out the low voices of Derek and the deliveryman. The package was for her. She suddenly knew it without a shred of doubt.

Felix had tracked her to the Colton ranch.

Chloe's hands shook so wildly she laid her palms flat on her thighs, trying to control the trembling. At the gate, Derek exchanged a few more words with the FedEx man, who wore a look of apprehension mingled with annoyance. The man flipped through some papers on his clipboard, shaking his head repeatedly as Derek continued to unleash what looked like a serious interrogation. After a few moments, Derek's hand moved in a gesture of pure frustration and he stalked back to the car.

The driver returned to his truck, the engine roared and then the truck reversed away from the gate, raising a cloud of dust as it sped off.

Derek slid back into the driver's seat without a word, twisted around and placed the package in the backseat.

"It's for me, isn't it?" she said softly.

He nodded.

"Addressed to Amelia Phillips?" she prompted.

He shook his head.

"Chloe Moreno?" she whispered.

"Yes."

A chill seized her insides, making her tremble again. It was over. Felix knew she was alive. Oh, God—and he knew she was staying at the Colton ranch. He knew about Derek.

Her voice cracked as she asked, "Who sent it?"

"There was no sender information," he answered in a clipped tone. "Whoever it was used a FedEx office in Philly and paid in cash."

Panic clawed up Chloe's throat like a scavenger tearing apart a carcass. Her heart pounded, each beat thudding in her ears until all she could hear was that wild, frantic rhythm. Neither she nor Derek said another word as he drove to his house.

As if the weather had decided to match her mood, a gust of icy wind slammed into her when she got out of the car. Derek grabbed the package from the backseat and they silently marched up to the porch. In the front hall they removed their coats in silence, left their boots on the shoe rack lining the floor then walked into the living room without a word.

Derek held out the package and finally spoke. "Would you like me to open it?"

"No." She gulped. "I'll do it."

The cardboard box was the size of a shoebox. Chloe tested its weight and found that it was lighter than it looked. The recipient data glared up at her like an accusation. Typed out and printed on a sticker, it listed the name Chloe Moreno, with Derek's address underneath it. After a few seconds of hesitation, she peeled the tape from the edges of the box and slowly opened the two flaps of cardboard.

The blood drained from her face as she laid eyes on the contents of the box.

"What is it?" Derek demanded.

She continued to stare at the box, tears welling up in her eyes. The slice of cake was a thing of beauty, milky white butter cream icing, gorgeous pale pink roses done in painstaking detail. Last time she'd seen it, it had been covered by a layer of freezer burn. Now, the cake looked the way it had at her wedding: creamy, decadent, utterly beautiful.

One tear slipped out and snaked down her cheek. Without a word, she handed the box to Derek. "It's a piece of my wedding cake," she said dully. "Felix preserved one slice and kept it in our freezer in Malibu."

A sense of numbness washed over her, her vision becoming nothing but a gauzy haze. Through that haze, she saw Derek examine the cake. Saw him set the box on the coffee table. Saw him approach her. But just as he came near, just as he reached out his hand, that numb feeling transformed into a hot rush of emotion and the last thread of control snapped inside her like an elastic band.

"I have to go," she blurted out.

Derek blinked. "What are you talking about?"

But she was beyond listening. As alarms shrieked in her head like a banshee, she tore out of the living room and stumbled into the guest room. Her lungs burned, but sucking in sharp gulps of oxygen only made her feel light-headed. Panting, she whirled around the room like a madwoman, gathering the few belongings she'd unpacked and shoving them into her duffel bag.

"What are you doing?" Derek demanded.

She spun around to find him standing in the doorway, a worried expression creasing his features.

"I'm leaving," she snapped.

"Chloe—"

She rushed into the guest bath and grabbed her toothbrush and makeup kit, then hurried back to the room. "I can't stay here," she mumbled through ragged breaths. "He'll come after me, Derek. He'll come after me and hurt me and I can't be hurt again and—"

She couldn't finish. Her throat felt too tight, and her legs could no longer support her.

God, she was having a heart attack.

Panic torpedoed into her, causing her to sink onto the edge of the bed. Her palms tingled, her vision nothing but a whirlwind of black-and-white dots. Gasping for air, Chloe dropped her head between her knees, but her heart only seemed to beat faster. So fast she feared it might burst right out of her chest.

She nearly toppled off the bed when she felt Derek's hand on her back. "Breathe," he said urgently, his hands rubbing circular motions between her shoulder blades. "Come on, sweetheart, breathe."

Her vision swam again. "I can't," she choked out.

"Yes, you can." His fingers threaded in her hair. "You're having a panic attack. You're hyperventilating, and you need to breathe."

She tried. Inhaled. Exhaled. Over and over again, until her breaths grew less shallow and her head began to clear.

"That's it," Derek murmured. "Keep breathing."

She kept breathing.

It took several minutes before her heartbeat regulated. Before she could lift her head and see everything clearly again. But while the anxiety attack had ebbed, her determination to escape remained strong.

"I have to go," she said firmly. "He had that cake delivered to the ranch, Derek. That means he knows I'm staying with you. That means you and your family are in danger now."

"My family and I will be fine," he replied, wrapping one arm around her trembling shoulders. "And you're not going anywhere, Chloe."

"I have to." Misery hung from her tone. "I can't let him hurt me again."

"He won't hurt you."

She gazed into Derek's brown eyes, but not even the conviction she saw in them could ease her terror. "He already did. He hurt me so badly."

"I know he did, sweetheart."

"No. No, you don't." Fury blasted into her. "You don't know what he did to me, Derek. You don't know a damn thing."

His gaze filled with shock. "Chloe—"

"Do you want to see how much he hurt me? Do you?"

"Chloe—"

She shot to her feet and grabbed the makeup bag she'd left on top of her duffel. She didn't know why she was so enraged, why her eyes kept shooting daggers in Derek's direction. None of this was his fault, yet she couldn't seem to control the fury traveling like poison through her veins. The urge to lash out was too powerful, the need to flee even more so.

Her fingers shook as she unzipped the bag and fumbled for the tube of makeup remover and cleansing cloths.

As her mouth twisted bitterly, she walked over to the mirror hanging over the low dresser across the room. In the reflection, she saw Derek rise from the bed. He approached her the way one would approach a rabid animal. "What are you doing?" he asked gently.

"Showing you what he did to me."

She began removing the makeup. Foundation and concealer and powder and toner disappeared like the top layer of paint on a canvas, revealing the secret image beneath the surface. Only, her transformation didn't uncover a lost masterpiece. Hers showed the ugliness beneath the mask she wore.

After she'd wiped her cheek clean, she clenched her teeth and turned to face Derek.

His eyes widened, but the disgust she'd expected to see didn't come. If anything, he looked so incredibly sad.

"Felix did that to you?" he murmured.

"Let's see if men still find you attractive now, shall we?"

"Yes." She quickly spun around, needing to avert her eyes,

but Derek's gaze found her in the reflection of the mirror, making it impossible to hide from him.

The scar didn't look as gruesome as it had a year ago. No longer an angry red, it was now pinkish-white, but that didn't bring her any relief because that pinkish-white line still evoked the same rush of shame. Starting right beneath her left eyebrow, the scar slashed diagonally across her cheek, then curved, ending right in the center of her chin. Derek might not be disgusted by it, but Chloe sure as hell was. The mere sight of that scar made her want to scream and curse and strike at anything in her path.

"We were at a hospital charity benefit," she said, unable to take her eyes off her own face. "I was mingling, playing the part of his perfect little wife. Several men flirted with me, but I made sure not to provoke Felix by being overly friendly. He was always insanely jealous, and I'd learned early on not to show more than polite interest toward other men. But that night this businessman kept trying to paw at me. He was coming on strong, and Felix didn't like it one bit."

Tears leaked from the corners of her eyes, following the path of her scar down to her chin. Derek took a step closer and stood behind her, his handsome face creased with unhappiness as they watched each other in the mirror.

"He didn't cause a scene during the party. He just announced we were leaving early, got our coats and led me outside. He didn't drive home. Instead, we drove to his office building." Acid coated her throat. "He said he needed to pick up something he forgot. So we went up to his office and that's when he freaked out. He called me a whore and accused me of encouraging the men at the party to flirt with me."

She swallowed hard. "He kept saying how pretty I was, how I used my beauty to manipulate men. And then he just exploded. He told me no man but him was allowed to look at me, and that he would make sure no one found me attractive ever again. So he grabbed a scalpel and..."

She bit her lip, trying to find the courage to continue, but Derek didn't let her. In the blink of an eye, he yanked her into his arms and held her so tightly she couldn't draw a breath.

"I'm so sorry, sweetheart." His breath warmed the top of her head. "I'm so very sorry."

Chloe wanted to stay in his arms forever. He smelled so damn good, felt so damn solid. Derek Colton truly was a rock—she now knew why his family depended on him so much, why everyone in the community turned to this man when they needed help, support, advice.

But as much as she wanted to lose herself in his protective embrace, she refused to risk Derek's life.

"That's why I have to go," she whispered, reluctantly stepping out of his arms. "Felix is capable of anything. If he could do this—" she gestured to her cheek "—to his own wife, then he wouldn't hesitate to hurt you, a complete stranger."

Fighting a new dose of fear, she sucked in a breath and hurried toward her duffel bag. "I'm leaving."

"Running," he said flatly.

She tightened her jaw. "Yes. I'm running, okay?"

"Without even securing a new identity?"

"There's no time." She zipped up her bag and slung the strap over her shoulder. "He knows I'm at the ranch and I need to go before he decides to show up for whatever twisted end game he's got planned."

"Chloe." Derek sighed. "Be reasonable. You're panicked. Scared. You can't make impulsive decisions in this condition. You need to be smart about this. So put down the bag, come into the kitchen and we'll make some coffee and come up with a plan."

The fear swimming in her belly wouldn't let her consider the suggestion. She marched to the door, stopping only to shoot him a look loaded with sorrow and regret. "I'm leaving, Derek."

When he made a move toward her, she held up her hand. "Please," she begged. "Please don't try to stop me."

"I wasn't going to."

She stared at him in bewilderment. "What?"

His face hardened in fortitude. "If you're so damn determined to go, then I'm coming with you."

Chapter 9

Derek was calling Chloe's bluff. Well, not so much calling her bluff as waiting for her to come to her senses.

He knew she was acting on pure instinct, driven by fear rather than rational thought. The latest delivery had left her feeling as if she'd been backed into a corner, and faced with the choice of fighting or fleeing, she'd chosen the latter. But Derek knew that any second now she'd realize what a mistake this was. The way she'd executed her escape from Felix with careful consideration and diligent preparation told Derek that this woman was a planner. No way would she skip town half-cocked without any semblance of a plan.

And so he sat quietly in the passenger seat of Chloe's hatchback, watching her from the corner of his eye as she followed the river that ran along the edge of town. He doubted she even had a destination in mind; she seemed to be driving aimlessly through Eden Falls, which told him she was beginning to see the situation with clarity.

It still floored him that she was doing all this to protect *him.* Yes, she feared for her own life, but it was the thought of her husband hurting Derek and his family that had pushed her over the edge. He couldn't remember the last time a woman had worried about *his* well-being. Tess had been so focused on herself he hadn't even made a blip on her radar.

But Chloe? She'd been downright inconsolable from the notion that he might get hurt. Ironically, he felt the same damn way—the mere thought of Chloe getting hurt sliced at his insides like a razor blade.

Derek shot her a sidelong look, feeling utterly bewildered. Her delicate profile, those straight white teeth worrying her plush bottom lip, her blond hair falling over one shoulder…the woman was so beautiful she took his breath away.

Ever since he'd nearly made love to her—on his desk, for Pete's sake—he'd been fighting the need to kiss her again. The urge to strip off her clothes and explore every inch of her tempting body. The little moans she'd made when she'd come apart from his touch continued to echo in his head, and he'd been in a state of hot arousal ever since yesterday afternoon.

The primal need to claim this woman had left him unhinged. He'd never felt this way before, not even with Tess. Chloe unleashed a passionate side he'd never possessed with his wife, and he had no idea how to deal with it. All he knew was that he wanted her. *Craved* her.

At the same time, he didn't want to make any promises he wasn't sure he could keep. He didn't want to hurt her with his inability to open his heart. Christ, she'd been hurt so much already.

His gaze was drawn to her cheek, the smooth ivory skin flushed with a pinkish hue. She was facing straight ahead to watch the road, so Derek couldn't see the scar, but the memory of it had been burned into his brain.

Fury clamped around his spine and he had to wrench his gaze away in case she caught a glimpse of his expression. What kind of monster took a scalpel to the face of the woman he claimed to love? Felix Moreno was damn lucky Derek wasn't standing in front of him at this very moment—because Derek would have strangled that sick bastard to death, his oath to heal and protect be damned.

"Aw, hell."

Chloe's anguished mumble jarred him back to the present.

He turned to look at her, hiding a smile as she slowed the car and pulled onto the shoulder of the road.

"What am I doing?" she said with a heavy sigh.

"Come to your senses, did ya?" He couldn't control the teasing note in his voice.

"Remind me never to make impulsive decisions during a panic attack," she said wryly.

Before he could respond, she reached for the door handle. "I need air."

They got out of the car and Chloe drifted toward the gentle slope that overlooked the river below. Derek came up beside her, and, after a moment of hesitation, placed his hand on her arm. "You okay?"

She offered a faint laugh. "Not really." She paused, focusing on the riverbank. "Let's walk."

He blinked. "Now?"

"Yes." Without waiting for his answer, she began descending the slope, her black leather boots sinking into the two-inch layer of snow covering the grass.

Deciding to humor her, Derek zipped up his coat and followed her down the slope. It was a cool evening, dark and chilly, but at least it wasn't snowing. The moon sat high in the sky, illuminating the river as they made their way to the muddy, pebble-strewn bank.

Chloe didn't say a word as she walked. Her breath left white billows in the air. Her cheeks were as red as her scarf, but she didn't seem to mind the cold. Derek let her take the lead, realizing immediately where she was heading. Eden Falls River culminated in the serene waterfall that the town had been named after, but Derek hadn't been there in years. It was too close to the bridge where he'd lost Tess, a site he avoided as often as possible.

"I have two options," Chloe said suddenly.

"Which are?" Because she was walking ahead of him, he

couldn't see her expression, but the droop of her shoulders revealed her unhappiness.

"I can disappear. For good this time. No nursing, no public life. Just get a new identity, leave the country and hide for the rest of my life."

Twigs and frost crackled beneath their boots as they approached the spot where the river narrowed and the landscape dipped. The sound of rushing water hissed in the air, and then the waterfall came into view. It was wider than it was tall, and Derek had never seen it go dry or freeze, not even in the hottest of summers or coldest of winters. Just like the water washing over the boulders at the fall's base, a sense of peace washed over him. He rarely had the time to be out in nature these days; his practice was too busy, his family too demanding. As he glanced at Chloe's strained profile, he wished that they were here under different circumstances.

"But I don't want to do that," she said, referring to the option she'd raised. "I don't want to hide away, Derek. And then there's my dad—I can't leave him. He might not remember me, but I still want to be close by if he needs me."

"What's the second option?" Derek asked.

"Go back to California."

Every muscle in his body went taut. "Go back to Felix?" he demanded.

She quickly shook her head. "Go back and face him," she clarified. "I'll hire a lawyer and a bodyguard. File for divorce, get a restraining order and then maybe I'll move to Missouri to be near my dad." A shaky breath left her mouth, staining the air white. "I'll just have to be careful, never go anywhere alone and pray that Felix doesn't decide to come after me."

"And live your life constantly looking over your shoulder, waiting for him to make a move," Derek said grimly.

Her pretty features creased with desperation. "What other choice do I have? Faking my death clearly wasn't enough, and I don't want to sit on some beach in South America until the end of time. My dad is safe thanks to that bodyguard you hired, which means Felix can't use him as a way to lure me back." She sighed. "I just want this to be over. If that means confronting Felix and getting cops and lawyers involved, then I think I have to do that."

The thought of Chloe confronting her violent husband cut into his gut like a dull blade.

"I'm tired of running," she murmured. "And I'm tired of being afraid."

His throat tightened, making it difficult to get a word out. He wanted to tell her that she could stay at the ranch—forever, if she wanted. But he knew she'd never agree. This evening's delivery confirmed that Felix had tracked her to the Double C, and Derek knew that Chloe would rather die herself than let Felix hurt anyone living on the ranch.

"I'll make arrangements to leave in the morning," she finished in a soft voice.

"No."

Her brows furrowed. "Derek—"

"Stay," he interrupted.

"I can't."

He bridged the few feet of distance between them and cupped her chin with his hands. His thumb swept over the pronounced scar tissue on her cheek, and a feeling of pure protectiveness seized his heart. Damn it, he didn't want her to go. It stunned him to realize how deeply he'd come to care about Chloe in the month he'd known her. How much he'd come to depend on her. How much he looked forward to seeing her every day.

What he felt for her went beyond sexual attraction. She... *soothed* him. Being around Chloe brought him a sense of calm that he hadn't felt in years.

"You can't just hop on a plane to L.A. and confront that son of a bitch," Derek said in a low voice. "You need to contact a lawyer first, hire a guard, make arrangements. Stay at the ranch for a few more days, at least until you figure it all out, and when the time comes for you to face Felix, I'll do it with you."

Her breath hitched. "What? Why would you do that?"

"Because I refuse to let you confront that maniac alone." Anger rippled through him, intensifying when the pad of his thumb brushed her scar. "I won't let him hurt you again, sweetheart."

Disbelief echoed in her voice. "You want to come to California with me? What about your family? Your patients?"

"They can survive without me for a week or two," he said firmly.

"A week or two?" she echoed. "You're planning on taking that much time off?"

"You think I'm going to hold your hand while you see your husband for the first time in months and then abandon you? No way. I'll stick around for as long as I can, and if you do plan on moving to St. Louis, I'll help you make those arrangements, too." A thought occurred to him. "Or you could move your father to a facility in Philadelphia. That way you could continue working at the clinic. With me."

Amazement washed over her face. "Why are you doing all of this, Derek? I know you said you want to be friends, but this is above and beyond—"

"Friends?" he cut in. A laugh rumbled out of his chest. "I was lying through my damn teeth when I said that. I don't want to be your friend, Chloe. I want…I want *this*."

His lips covered hers in a hard kiss.

Their tongues tangled, breaths mingled, chests collided. Desire swamped his body as he explored her mouth, and his erection strained against the zipper of his trousers, pleading for attention. When Chloe ground her lower body into his, he growled with sheer masculine pleasure and deepened the kiss, while his hands fumbled with the buttons of her coat.

He was about to push the wool fabric off her slender shoulders when he realized where they were. The frigid air cooled

some of the heat streaking through his veins, helping him regain his senses. "Let's go back to the car," he rasped.

"It's too far away," she said breathlessly.

Then she kissed him again, and his surroundings faded
away. The only thing that registered was her warm mouth,
her curvy body straining into his, her impatient hands claw-
ing at his zipper.

Groaning, Derek flung off his coat and spread it on the cold
earth, then he sank to his knees, bringing Chloe down with
him. He'd never experienced such all-consuming lust, such
overwhelming anticipation. He needed this woman the way
he needed his next breath, and she seemed to be infected by
that same mad rush of need.

She lay on her back and yanked him on top of her, their
mouths finding each other once more. Her fingers undid his fly.
His fingers tugged on the waistband of her snug black pants.
He peeled the stretchy material down her legs, cursing when
he saw the goose pimples rise on her bare flesh.

"It's too cold," he mumbled.

"Then warm me up," she mumbled back.

Derek brought one hand between her legs, groaning when he
felt how wet she was. As his heart pounded out a wild rhythm
in his chest, he stroked her slick folds, summoning a soft moan
from her lush lips. He was too wound up for foreplay, too desperate to get inside her. He rubbed his palm over her core, once,
twice, then slid a finger into her wet heat. Lord, she was tight.

With another growl, he eased his pants and boxers down
his hips, positioned his throbbing erection and drove into her.

"God. *Derek.*"

Chloe let out a husky cry and bucked her hips to bring him
deeper.

Derek couldn't have controlled his strokes if his life depended on it. There was nothing slow or tender about their
lovemaking—it was frantic, uncontrollable, a wild race to the

finish line. Chloe clung to his shoulders as he plunged into her, moaned, whispered his name, urged him to go faster.

His pulse raced as he made love to her with rough, shallow strokes. Hips pistoning, chest heaving, pleasure gathering in his groin and fogging his head. He registered the glazed look in Chloe's hazel eyes and knew she felt that same sense of bliss and desperation.

"More," she choked out, lifting her hips again. "Please, Derek, I need more."

He moved even faster, sliding his hands beneath her black turtleneck sweater to squeeze her breasts over her bra. The second his palms touched those firm mounds, Chloe started to convulse, crying out from the orgasm.

Her inner muscles clenched around his cock like a hot vise, sending him teetering right over the edge. As his climax ripped through him with the force of a hurricane, Derek buried his face in the crook of her neck and breathed in the heady scent of her. His hips kept moving, bursts of pleasure igniting every inch of his body.

Eventually they both grew still, and Derek became aware of the chill nipping at his bare ass. Unable to stop himself, he let out a deep laugh.

Chloe's eyes flew open. "Are you laughing at me?"

Another chuckle squeezed out of his lungs. "Not at you. At *us*."

He slowly withdrew from her tight channel, immediately experiencing a sense of loss. And he suddenly realized that in their passion, they'd neglected to use any protection.

Chloe must have realized it at the same time because she shot him a reassuring look. "I'm not at the right part of my cycle," she murmured. Her voice cracked. "Besides, I'm not sure I can even get pregnant anymore."

The pain in her eyes brought an ache to his chest. Not wanting to spoil this perfect moment with past heartache, he flashed her a grin and said, "We're animals, Chloe. We didn't even make it to the damn car."

Now she was laughing, too. She propped herself up on her elbows and glanced around, as if noticing for the first time that they were lying on the rocky ground next to the small pool at the base of the waterfall.

Then her gaze shifted back to his face and her expression softened. "You know what? I'm glad this happened here." Her throat dipped as she swallowed. "I feel…safe here. Happy." The smile she bestowed him made Derek's heart squeeze with joy. "No matter what happens, I'll always think of this waterfall as my safe place, Derek."

Overcome with emotion, he lowered his head and kissed her. "Me, too, sweetheart. Me, too."

Over the next three days, Chloe and Derek fell into a routine that alternated between work and sex, with the occasional dinner with Sawyer thrown in. They'd told Derek's younger siblings that Chloe was staying at the ranch while her apartment was being fumigated, and neither kid had questioned it. Sawyer, in particular, had been thrilled to discover that Chloe was Derek's houseguest.

Although she knew she ought to be making plans to return to California and officially divorce Felix, it was so hard to focus on the dark cloud hanging over her head when Derek had brought a ray of sunshine into her life.

There was no doubt about it—she was smitten. She hadn't thought the word *smitten* could apply to a woman her age, but it was the only way to describe how she felt about Derek. Being with him was a whole new experience for her. He listened to her, treated her with respect, complimented her, made her laugh.

And the man couldn't keep his hands off her. Not that Chloe was complaining—she couldn't keep her hands off him, either. These past three days, they'd made love every morning before work and every night when they got home from the clinic. Derek had even woken her up at four o'clock this morning, his brown eyes glimmering with sinful promise as he'd slipped his hand between her legs and proceeded to bring her to orgasm before making slow, sweet love to her.

She'd never felt more sexually sated in her life, and ever since Derek had lowered his guard and made love to her, he seemed so much more relaxed, so much happier.

God, she was happy, too, and it broke her heart, knowing this feeling wouldn't last. She hadn't received any more gifts from her husband, but she knew Felix hadn't just up and left town. No, he must be planning a new attack, figuring out a new way to hurt her. Which meant she couldn't keep pretending the threat didn't exist.

"We need to make some plans," she said, shooting a pointed look at the driver's seat.

Derek kept his eyes on the road, but his profile revealed his slight frown. "I know," he responded.

They'd taken the morning off in order to drive to Philadelphia General, where Derek's Amish patient Rachel was scheduled to have her biopsy done. Derek hadn't wanted Chloe to go, but she'd insisted; she'd promised Rachel and her husband that she'd be there for them today, and she couldn't bring herself to disappoint them. In the end, Derek had announced that if she was going, he'd go with her, and he'd promptly canceled his morning appointments. It touched her, the way he refused to let her out of his sight.

But that wouldn't last forever, either. Eventually, she would have to say goodbye to Derek, a reminder that never failed to bring a dull ache to her heart.

"I placed another call to my contact last night," she told him. "He's emailing me the names of some bodyguards he recommends. A lot of them are former military, and he says they're very good."

Derek's jaw tensed.

"I think I'll contact the lawyer who handled my parents' affairs," she went on. "He'll be able to help me with the divorce and the restraining order."

He still didn't respond.

"I'll check the airlines for cheap flights tonight." She hesitated. "I know you said you want to go to L.A. with me, but—"

"But nothing," he interrupted, an edge to his voice. "I'll be sitting right beside you on that plane, sweetheart."

Unease and joy warred inside her. As much as she wanted Derek by her side, she didn't want to drag him into this mess. He had a life in Eden Falls. His practice, his family. It didn't feel right asking him to drop everything just so he could hold her hand while she tried to exorcise Felix from her life.

But something she'd learned over the past few days was that Derek Colton was stubborn as a mule. Not to mention sweet, loving, funny.

Incredible in bed…

Flushing, she suddenly pictured Derek's gorgeous face taut with passion while his muscular body moved over hers, and a shiver danced up her spine. She couldn't get enough of Derek Colton, especially now that she'd discovered that beneath the calm, professional exterior was a man far more sensual than she'd ever imagined.

"We'll talk about the details later," he added as he drove into the visitor's parking lot in front of the hospital entrance.

After Derek got a parking slip and tucked it on the dashboard, they headed into the modern gray building and walked toward the elevator. They were meeting the Danfords in the oncology wing, which made Chloe gulp. The word *oncology* sounded so ominous, a grim reminder that the mass in Rachel Danford's breast could very well end up being malignant.

The Danfords seemed to be thinking along the same lines when Chloe and Derek entered the waiting room next to the nurses' station; the young Amish couple looked so upset that Chloe made a beeline for Rachel.

Pasting an encouraging smile on her face, Chloe squeezed the young woman's hand. "Everything is going to be fine," she said softly.

Rachel bit on her plump bottom lip. "I hope so." Noticing Derek, the woman frowned. "Dr. Colton? What are you doing here?" Her face paled. "Is there something wrong?"

"Nothing is wrong," Derek said with a gentle smile. "I came by for moral support."

The young woman looked genuinely touched, as did her husband, Jacob, who approached to shake hands with Derek.

"Did Dr. Greenleigh explain the procedure to you?" Derek asked as they all sat down.

The couple nodded.

"Did you have any questions or concerns that you wanted to talk about?"

Jacob hesitated. "Dr. Greenleigh did not say if we would know the results right away."

"It depends," Derek answered. "Sometimes the doctor can immediately diagnose the sample as benign. The samples are analyzed after their withdrawal and the doctor can determine if they came from a cyst or whatnot. In most cases, the tissue and fluid samples need to be analyzed in the lab by a pathologist."

"Will it hurt?" Rachel whispered. She reached out and clutched Chloe's hand.

"They'll inject local anesthesia to make sure there's no discomfort," Derek assured her. "And there'll only be a small nick where the needle will be inserted. It'll be over before you know it, Rachel."

Rachel tightened her grip on Chloe's hand. "Thank you for being here," she said. "Will you come into the room with me for the procedure?"

Jacob ran a frustrated hand over his long beard. "I want to be there with you," he said stiffly.

Rachel's voice was surprisingly firm. "No, my husband. I don't want you there." Her tone brooked no argument, and

Chloe suspected that banishing her husband to the waiting room was more about protecting Jacob than any embarrassment on Rachel's part.

Amish women were tough as nails, which was something Chloe had learned through her interaction with their Amish patients. The women of Paradise Ridge woke up at the crack of dawn to do their chores, raise their children, support their husbands—and they did it all without the benefit of technology. Most women these days couldn't last a day without their cell phones or blow dryers or whatever technological luxuries they depended on, but women like Rachel Danford were of a different breed. Strong, resilient, awe-inspiring. Chloe knew Jacob's instinct was to protect his wife, but from the calm expression in Rachel's eyes, it was obvious she could weather anything, even a potentially malignant tumor.

When Dr. Greenleigh entered the waiting room a few minutes later, both Rachel and Chloe stood up. Rachel did not kiss or embrace her husband, but she placed her palm on his chest, right over his heart. Chloe's gaze unconsciously shifted to Derek, who was watching the couple with a tender expression.

Their eyes locked, and her pulse sped up. Why did he have to be so damn appealing? Each time he looked at her with those deep brown eyes, said something in his husky baritone voice, touched her with those big, capable hands, she utterly melted. Lord, she could so easily fall in love with this man if she let herself. But she couldn't. She *wouldn't*. Her future was one big unknown, and she refused to drag Derek into the mess that her life would surely become once she returned to California.

"This way," Dr. Greenleigh said, gesturing to the door. The oncologist was a tall, slender brunette with kind green eyes and an efficient manner. She led Rachel and Chloe into the exam room, then left while Rachel changed into a hospital gown.

The entire procedure was over in less than an hour. Rachel had put on a brave face, but Chloe knew the woman was still shaken up, especially when Dr. Greenleigh said it would take several days for the results to come in. After the nurse applied a compression dressing to Rachel's incision area, she quickly got dressed. She and Chloe returned to the waiting room, where Jacob immediately clasped his wife's hand as if he never wanted to let her out of his sight again.

Chloe and Derek quietly slipped out of the room. As they strode down the fluorescent-lit corridor, Derek surprised her by taking her hand.

"She did a good job," Chloe told him. "She's incredibly strong."

He shot her a sidelong look. "So are you. I think you've got the biggest heart of anyone I've ever met."

Pleasure flooded her womb. She wanted to tell him that she felt stronger when he was around, but that sounded too sappy. Instead, she laced her fingers through his and tried not to grin like a schoolgirl. Derek's husky compliments were liable to give her an ego.

They reached the end of the hall, and just as they turned the corner, Chloe spotted a familiar face by the elevator.

All the air left her lungs in one dizzying swoop.

With a jolt of panic, she darted back around the corner, pressing her back against the white wall as her heart hammered into her ribs.

Derek appeared in front of her, looking bewildered. "What's wrong?" he demanded.

She tried to control the unbridled gallop of her pulse. Inhaled deeply. Exhaled in a long rush. Ignoring Derek, she crept along the wall and chanced another peek around the corner.

Still there.

A hysterical laugh lodged in her throat. Not a figment of her imagination, then. No, just the star of nightmares.

Standing on the other end of the corridor, his seductive dark eyes twinkling as he flirted with a nurse and his broad shoulders filling his white coat to perfection, was none other than her husband.

Chapter 10

Derek had no idea what was going on. One second Chloe was holding his hand and smiling, the next she'd plastered herself against the wall, her face white as a sheet.

"What's going on?" he demanded, glancing around the corridor. He half expected a crazed killer to pop out of one of the doorways, covered in blood and wielding a chain saw. But the hallway was empty.

Chloe fisted the front of his sweater, clutching at the fabric. She looked eerily pale, and her voice sounded tinny as she said, "Felix."

Derek's brows knitted. "What are you talking about?"

"Felix," she hissed again. "He's here." One finger pointed to the end of the hall, and then her arm dropped limply to her side. "He's *here*."

His frown deepened. "Are you sure?"

"Of course I'm sure. I was married to the man for twelve years," she snapped. "I think I know what he looks like."

Derek blinked in surprise. Chloe had never snapped at him like that before, which told him that she was seriously shaken up. Despite her shrill protest, he edged along the wall and snuck a peek around the corner. He immediately spotted the culprit responsible for putting that fearful expression in Chloe's hazel eyes.

Six feet tall, with slicked-back black hair and dark good-looks, the man standing by the elevator looked like a Latin heartthrob. He wore a simple white coat, but his tailored pin-stripe trousers and shiny black alligator loafers screamed of wealth. Charm oozed from his pores as he chatted with a petite, blond-haired nurse.

He stared at Felix Moreno in distaste, tempted to march down the hall and land an uppercut on the man's square jaw. Battling the urge, Derek ducked out of sight and returned to Chloe. She still looked stricken, her eyes wide with despair as she met Derek's gaze.

"I have to get out of here," she whispered.

He gave a sharp nod. "Take the stairwell," he ordered, gesturing to the doorway to their right. He reached into his pocket for his car keys and thrust them into her hand. "Wait in the car for me."

"What are you going to do?" she asked in alarm.

"Find out what he's doing here," Derek said curtly.

"You can't confront him," she protested. "Please, Derek. This isn't the time."

He ignored the plea. "Go wait in the car, Chloe. I'll be there in five minutes."

After a second of visible reluctance, she dashed toward the stairwell door and disappeared. He heard the muffled sound of her footsteps as she hurried down the stairs.

Fighting the impulse to go after Moreno, Derek walked in the opposite direction toward the oncology wing. At the nurses' station, he greeted the nurse at the desk, introduced himself and asked to use the phone. He quickly dialed the number of a colleague he'd once worked with when he'd done his residency in the hospital's downstairs emergency room. Burt Winters had chosen to streamline into the plastic surgery field and now worked as the department head, and Derek was suddenly very grateful for that fact.

When he got Winters on the line, the surgeon barked out a curt hello, his tone warming when Derek greeted him.

"Colton!" Winters sounded delighted. "I haven't spoken to you in ages. How's small-town doctor life?" A note of mocking derision tinkled over the extension.

Derek rolled his eyes. His colleague always teased him mercilessly for giving up his resident position here in order to open his own practice in Eden Falls. Winters claimed Derek had taken a step down, but Derek didn't view it that way. His practice allowed for a relationship with his patients that the emergency room had denied him. The E.R. was an endless stream of nameless, faceless people, with bedside manner thrown away in favor of swift efficiency and blink-of-the-eye decisions. Chaos was the norm, gratitude rarely given. Opening the clinic in Eden Falls had been the best decision Derek had ever made.

"It's great. Busy, too. Who would've thought that small-town folks get as sick as city folks?" Derek answered good-naturedly.

Winters laughed. "What can I do for you, Colton?"

"I'm actually calling for some information about a surgeon who's consulting on a case for you. I was told that—"

"Felix Moreno," Winters interrupted, a tad smug. "Yes, Moreno is assisting me on a reconstruction case. We scrub in this evening, in fact."

"What's the case?" Derek asked casually.

"Did you hear about the accident on Route 30 last week?"

"The four teenagers who died when they were hit by the drunk driver? Yeah, I saw it on the news."

"Three died," Winters corrected. "One of the girls survived. She's sixteen, and her face was crushed in the accident. It's a messy one, Colton, real messy. I contacted Moreno, didn't think I stood a chance in hell of getting him to agree to come—he's got a waiting list a mile long for consultations. But the case intrigued him, so he flew in a few days ago. We couldn't operate then because the patient came down with a secondary infection that needed to be treated first."

"Sounds like a tough case," Derek remarked.

"It is." Winters paused. "So why the interest in Moreno?"

"I have a patient who's considering rhinoplasty," Derek lied. "She saw Moreno on that TV special he was featured in, the one on the medical cable channel. Anyway, she's determined to do her surgery with him."

Winters snorted. "Good luck with that. Moreno only takes high-profile patients—celebrities, athletes, politicians. Or cases that will get him written up in medical journals, like the one he's consulting on for us."

"Yeah, that's what I figured. But I promised her I'd try to contact him."

"Well, come by this evening if you want. Moreno'll probably spare a few minutes to talk to you. In the very least, he'll give you a business card and tell you to contact his office."

"I might do that," he said. "Thanks, Burt."

Five minutes later, Derek made his way across the parking lot toward his car. Through the windshield he could see that Chloe's pretty face was as ashen as ever. She kept fiddling with her hands in her lap, barely glancing his way as he slid into the driver's seat.

"Well?" she asked dully.

He quickly told her what he'd discovered, but Chloe didn't look appeased. "He's not here to consult on a case!" she burst out. "He's here because he knows I'm alive. He's clearly using this patient as a cover."

Derek chewed on the inside of his cheek. "I don't know. Maybe his being in Philly is a coincidence."

She laughed harshly. "He's here for me, Derek."

"Then why not come after you? Why break into your apartment and take you on this walk down memory lane? If he wanted to confront you, wouldn't he have done it by now?"

Her chin jutted out stubbornly. "Felix loves to play games. It's his MO—toy with someone, get them crazy with fear, make them sweat while they wonder when and how he'll strike." Her breathing went shallow. "That's what he did the night of the charity benefit, when he made me think his anger had faded, only to attack me in his office with a scalpel!"

Derek reached out and touched her cheek. She didn't flinch, but she didn't seem comfortable as he ran his fingers over her skin. She'd covered the scar up with makeup again, but a part of him wished she hadn't. These past three days she hadn't bothered with the makeup, at least not when the two of them were alone. Maybe she was finally beginning to believe that the scar didn't disgust him, which he'd repeatedly assured her since their encounter at the waterfall.

The waterfall… It still stunned him, how powerful their joining had been, how wild, frantic, all-consuming. He and Tess hadn't been very spontaneous when it came to sex, and by the end of their marriage, they'd fallen into a sexual routine that had lacked passion and excitement. But with Chloe, the passion had been present from the very first second, and in the past three days, it had only grown stronger.

Working with her at the clinic had become pure agony— each time she smiled at him, each time her arm brushed his, he wanted to rip off her clothes and devour her. Which was completely out of character for him. The mild-mannered, composed and perfect Derek Colton didn't ravish women. He didn't lock up his clinic and spend his lunch hour making love in his office…yet, he'd done just that, hadn't he? The memory of Chloe stretched out on his desk, her eyes smoky with desire as he drove into her, sent a rush of molten heat straight to his groin.

He quickly tamped it down. *Now's not the time, buddy.* Nope, it sure wasn't, seeing as the star of his naughty memories was on the verge of a panic attack at the moment.

Derek locked his gaze with hers. "It might be a coincidence," he said again. "But that's not a chance I'm willing to take, okay? We have to assume Felix *does* know you're alive and that he's planning on coming after you."

"So what do we do?"

He pursed his lips in thought. "I'm coming back here tonight to speak with him."

Her jaw fell open. "What? No. You can't do that. What if he—"

"What if he what?" Derek cut in. "Kills me, right here at the hospital, in front of hundreds of witnesses?"

"He sent that package to the ranch," Chloe reminded him. "He knows who you are, Derek."

"Which is why I want to see him, in a public place, where I can gauge his reaction. He might be a good liar, but I've got a great bullshit meter. If he knows who I am and my connection to you, I'll know, Chloe."

"What is talking to him going to achieve? What will you even say?"

"I won't mention you, if that's what you're afraid of. I'll keep it general, talk about the surgery or something. I just want to see how he reacts, see if he lets anything slip." He set his jaw. "And if he does reveal that he knows you're alive, I'll make sure he understands he's never coming anywhere near you again."

Chloe's expression softened. "You don't have to play the part of protector with me, Derek. I can face Felix on my own."

He chuckled ruefully. "I can't *not* protect the people in my life. Ask my family—they'll tell you it's true."

Chloe seemed unhappy with his answer, but she didn't give him a chance to question her cloudy expression. "Let's get out of here," she said with a sigh.

With a nod, he started the engine, then glanced over at her. "Do you mind if we make a stop first? We still have some time before we reopen the clinic, and there's something I need to do."

"Sure."

Putting the car in Drive, Derek pulled out of the lot and drove toward the main street, until the hospital was nothing but a gray dot in the rearview mirror.

* * *

I can't not protect the people in my life.

Chloe couldn't erase Derek's words from her head as he drove through the streets of downtown Philly toward whatever mysterious destination he was taking her to. Although she was still shaken up from seeing Felix at the hospital, her husband's reappearance in her life wasn't the only burden weighing on her mind.

Did Derek view her simply as someone who needed protecting?

The thought troubled her. She didn't want to be the damsel that Sir Derek had to rescue. All she'd ever wanted in her life was to find a man who viewed her as an equal. A worthy partner. She'd thought she'd found that with Felix—during their courtship, he'd claimed to want a strong woman at his side, yet within a few years of marriage, he'd chipped away at her strength, molded her into a weak, obedient doormat he could control.

Derek didn't try to control her, but a part of her wondered if he'd still be attracted to her if she didn't need his help.

And yes, maybe she *did* need him, but the question was—did he need *her?* Had she brought anything valuable into his life, aside from fueling those protective instincts of his?

Chloe didn't get the opportunity to make sense of her thoughts as the car came to a halt. When she looked out the window, she saw that they'd stopped in front of the Butterfly Hearts Community Center.

She wrinkled her brow. "Butterfly Hearts—isn't that the name of your family's foundation?"

Derek nodded as he killed the engine. "The organization also funds several community facilities around the state. This center was built right before Mom and Dad died. It caters to inner-city children and offers day-care services to single parents who can't afford it."

Chloe examined her surroundings as they stepped out of

the car. The neighborhood he'd brought her to wasn't the prettiest; litter marred the uneven sidewalks, graffiti covered the bus shelters and brick walls of the derelict buildings lining the street, and many of the storefronts featured barred windows. The community center almost seemed out of place amid its poverty-tainted backdrop. A redbrick building with large, gleaming windows, it featured a tidy lawn, a smooth concrete path and a bright green door with the word *Welcome!* painted on in yellow.

When they stepped into a main lobby that smelled of freshly baked cookies and pine cleaner, it was clear that Derek visited this place often. The African-American woman behind the front desk greeted him with a beaming smile, as did several of the staff members who stopped to talk to them as Derek and Chloe made their way down the hall.

"I usually come by a few times a month to say hi to the kids," Derek explained. "But with all the chaos in town, the missing Amish girls, Violet's accident…" He looked guilty. "I haven't been here in more than a month."

They reached a set of double doors, which Derek held open for her. Chloe slid through the doorway and found herself in an enormous room with bright yellow walls. Long tables took up the center of the room, and a carpeted play area spanned the far wall. Toys cluttered the floor, a TV in the corner blasted out a Disney movie and children of all ages occupied the various stations.

"Is this the day care?" she asked, turning to Derek.

"Yeah, but it's not usually this busy," he replied. "The holiday break started today, so there's twice the number of kids."

"Dr. Colton!"

The high-pitched female cry nearly shattered Chloe's eardrums. Just as she recovered from the audio assault, a little blond tornado swirled before her eyes. Before she could blink, Derek swept the tiny child in his arms and playfully tugged on one of her pigtails.

Chloe's jaw dropped. She'd never seen Derek's eyes twinkle like that before—and the big smacking kiss he planted on the little girl's cheek was also out of character.

"Did ya miss me?" he teased as he set the energetic girl back on her feet.

"Uh-huh! Wanna see the picture I painted?"

"I would love to, but first I want you to meet my friend," Derek said. "Daisy, this is Chloe."

Chloe knelt down and stuck out her hand. "Hi, Daisy. It's nice to meet you."

After a beat, the girl, who looked about three or four, placed a chubby, sticky hand in Chloe's. "Hi, Cwo-ee!"

Chloe's heart melted just a bit. "I'd love to see your picture, too," she prompted.

Still holding Chloe's hand, Daisy dragged her to one of the tables. Chloe and Derek oohed and ahhed as the little girl showed off her picture, which featured a lot of red-and-pink streaks that were apparently meant to be ribbons.

Within a minute, other kids swarmed the table—and all of them were thrilled to see "Dr. Colton." No matter their age, Derek interacted flawlessly with the children. Teasing, joking, laughing.

Chloe did her best to pay attention to the kids Derek introduced her to, but a part of her couldn't wrench her eyes off the man. He gave a piggyback ride to a six-year-old boy named Jesse. He stuck his fingers in a dish of pink paint and helped Daisy paint another picture. He talked basketball with a pair of twelve-year-olds, and when they begged him to shoot some hoops in the gym like he did "last time," Chloe realized there was yet another side to Derek Colton she'd never known existed.

The quiet doctor, the reluctant rancher, the stern father figure, the sensual lover, the unceasing protector…and now, this funny, playful, attentive guy who played basketball with kids and finger painted with toddlers.

Oh, no, Chloe, don't even think it.

She tried to push away the thought before it could surface, but she wasn't fast enough.

You're falling in love with him.

Her heart began beating at double speed, then kicked up another notch when the realization truly sunk in.

She was falling in love with Derek.

Oh, God. Hadn't she specifically ordered herself *not* to do that?

Right, because that's how it works, idiot.

Gulping, Chloe sneaked another peek at Derek, who was laughing over something Daisy had said. He had a splotch of yellow paint on his clean-shaven, mocha-colored cheek and a big grin on his face, those straight white teeth gleaming in the bright lighting of the day care. He looked happier and more relaxed than she'd ever seen him, and the ease with which he handled himself around Daisy and the other kids startled Chloe beyond belief.

Yep, Derek Colton really was full of surprises.

And yep, she'd totally, irrefutably fallen in love with him.

Later that evening, Derek rode the elevator of Philly General once again. When the doors dinged open, he strode down the hall toward the O.R. Burt Winters had booked for the surgery. Winters had arranged for Derek to be admitted into the gallery, a special privilege because the surgery was closed to viewing to protect the underage patient's privacy. Though he had no desire to witness the famous Felix Moreno in action, Derek ended up catching the tail end of the surgery.

It killed to admit it, but Moreno was a damn good surgeon. His hands moved with graceful precision as he concentrated on his task. Because the gallery's sound system wasn't activated, Derek couldn't hear what was being said in the O.R. below, but it was clear that Moreno was in charge. The rest of the staff looked on in awe—Winters, the surgical intern, nursing staff, even the anesthesiologist gazed at Moreno as if he were a medical god.

Derek shook his head, wondering how such a talented healer could harbor so much evil. Abusing his wife, scarring her, tormenting her. Moreno hid his violent, sociopathic nature behind a mask of charm and skill. No wonder Chloe had been drawn to him when they'd first met.

At the thought of Chloe, Derek's mood grew even more troubled. She'd been quiet and distant ever since they'd visited the community center. He knew seeing Felix had shaken her up, and he suspected being surrounded by all those children hadn't improved her state of mind. Realizing the kids must have reminded her of her loss, he suddenly wished he hadn't brought her with him.

In the O.R., the surgery had wrapped up, prompting Derek to rise from his seat. His muscles were stiff as he slid out the door. This was it. He was about to meet the man who'd driven Chloe to the other end of the country, who'd hurt her so deeply it was a miracle she'd been able to recover.

Taking a breath, Derek turned the corner just as Burt Winters exited the O.R.

"Colton," Winters called, looking both exhausted and triumphant. "Did you see it? A thing of beauty, huh?"

"Dr. Moreno is incredibly talented," Derek conceded.

"He's a miracle worker," Winters corrected. The sandy-haired surgeon glanced over his shoulder. "Here he comes now. Felix, there's someone I'd like to introduce you to."

Derek's hands curled into fists as Felix Moreno approached with long, confident strides. Chloe's husband still wore his surgical scrubs, but he'd removed his cap and mask, revealing his pronounced, good-looking features and a head of thick, wavy black hair. His dark eyes flickered with indifference as he extended a hand to Derek.

"Felix Moreno," he said smoothly.

"Derek Colton. It's a pleasure to meet you, Dr. Moreno."

"Please call me Felix."

Derek noted that Moreno's expression hadn't changed in the slightest when Derek introduced himself. Because Chloe's wedding cake had been delivered to the Colton ranch, he'd been expecting a reaction from the other man. But...nothing. Not even a flicker of recognition.

"Are you a surgeon?" Moreno asked.

"No, Derek chickened out and went the GP route," Winters said with a chortle.

Derek swallowed his annoyance. "I run a clinic in Eden Falls," he told Moreno. "It's a small town about sixty miles west of here."

He waited, but yet again, zero reaction from Moreno. The man was good. If he was the one sending Chloe those wedding mementos, then he must know she was living in Eden Falls, yet Moreno's face remained a composed mask of polite interest.

"So what can I do for you, Derek?" he asked, a hint of impatience in his voice.

"I'll leave you two to chat," Winters spoke up. "Come by my office tomorrow morning, Felix. There's some paperwork that needs to be filled out before you head back to L.A."

After Winters hurried off, Derek and Moreno eyed each other once more, and Derek got the feeling the other man was appraising him. Ah. Perhaps Moreno *did* know who he was.

"That was impressive work in there," Derek said graciously.

Moreno nodded. "I know."

Arrogant, much?

Yet the man's obvious case of self-worship didn't come as a surprise.

"I have a patient who's considering elective surgery," Derek went on. "Rhinoplasty."

Another nod.

"She saw that television special you did about reconstructive surgery and is interested in securing you as her surgeon."

Now Moreno chuckled. "I'm afraid she'll have to join a very long list of people interested in my services."

"Yes, Burt mentioned you have quite the waiting list." Derek scanned his brain, trying to find a way to steer the conversation toward a route that would provide him with some answers. "My patient recently lost her husband, and she's really set on this surgery. She feels it'll provide her with a better quality of life and make it easier to meet someone new."

Moreno looked sympathetic. "Rhinoplasty can be a great way to boost one's self-esteem, but though I'm sorry for your patient's loss, I simply don't have the time to take on minor cases for out-of-state patients."

"I understand."

As Moreno lifted his hand to run his fingers through his black hair, a glint of gold winked in the corridor, drawing Derek's gaze to the man's ring finger.

He forced his expression to remain neutral, even as his pulse sped up.

Moreno still wore his wedding ring.

Slanting his head in a casual pose, Derek gestured to the man's hand. "Are you married, Felix?"

Almost instantly the man's dark eyes went shuttered. "I was."

"Divorced?" Derek said, injecting sympathy into his voice.

"My wife died six months ago."

"I'm sorry to hear that. How long were you two married?"

"Twelve years." Moreno spoke in a flat pitch. "She is— *was*—a very difficult woman to love, but we made it work."

She is. Derek hadn't missed the present tense Moreno had initially used. Some people had a hard time switching to the past tense after losing a loved one, so that could've been a genuine slipup on Moreno's part.

Or it could be something else entirely.

He expected Moreno to change the subject, maybe stalk off with a brusque "Sorry, I can't help your patient," but to his unease, the surgeon pinned him down with a sharp stare. "What about you, Derek? Any special woman in your life?"

His guard shot up ten feet. "Not at the moment," he answered with a little shrug.

Moreno's dark eyes narrowed. "And why is that? I can't imagine your little practice keeping you very busy. You don't have anyone significant to pass the time with?"

Ignoring the jab at his practice, Derek kept his tone vague. "I'm afraid not."

"Well, I'm sorry to hear that." Moreno's tone relaxed. "Now, I must be going. I'd like to discuss the surgery with the patient's family. I imagine they'll be wanting to thank me."

Derek watched Chloe's husband stride off, unable to curb the apprehension coursing through him. The man was exactly how Chloe had described—the grandiose sense of self-importance, the superficial charm and slight narcissism. Moreno was too polished, too arrogant, and Derek could easily see him being a cruel, controlling perfectionist.

But he couldn't get an accurate read on the man. Some of Moreno's pointed remarks hinted that he knew about Chloe, but he hadn't given enough away for Derek to be sure.

So the question now was—how did they go about finding out exactly what Felix Moreno knew?

"Hit me," Sawyer said, staring at the cards on the table with a look of extreme concentration.

Chloe flipped over another card, revealing the five of hearts. She placed it next to the queen of spades and looked at Sawyer expectantly. "Fifteen. What do you say, Squirt?"

He scowled at her. "Hey, I said you can't call me Squirt. Only Derek can."

"Tough," she teased. "I like the nickname and I'm using it."

"Fine," he grumbled. "Um…hit me."

She flipped over another five. "Twenty."

"I'll stay," Sawyer said solemnly.

"Wise choice, sir. And dealer has…twenty-three. Bust. You win again."

As Sawyer collected the massive pile of toothpicks in the center of Derek's kitchen table, Chloe shuffled the cards, surprisingly happy that Sawyer had decided to stick around after Derek left for the hospital.

The boy had eaten dinner with them, then pleaded with Chloe to teach him how to play blackjack. It was the first time she'd been alone with Sawyer since she'd moved to town, but she no longer felt right keeping her distance from the boy, especially after he'd accused her of not liking children. As painful as it was to be around him sometimes, she'd decided to make an effort to get to know Derek's little brother, and now she was glad she had.

With Derek off meeting Felix, Chloe's nerves were strung tight, and Sawyer's presence helped keep her worries at bay.

Lord, her lover was meeting her husband.

It sounded like the plot of a tawdry soap opera, yet Chloe couldn't bring herself to feel guilty about her involvement with Derek. Her marriage to Felix had ended a long time ago. They may have been living together as husband and wife, but there had been no love. No tenderness. Not even mutual respect. Married to Felix, she'd stopped feeling like a woman. Because to him, she *hadn't* been a woman—she'd been his possession, his punching bag.

With Derek, she'd never felt more feminine in her life.

Yet at the same time, that scary truth she'd reached at the community center earlier today continued to haunt her. How could she have fallen for Derek? She'd *known* they'd have to say goodbye once she left to straighten out the mess her life had become, and she also knew that any feelings on her part were one-sided. Derek might enjoy her company, he might desire her, but love?

No, she suspected what he felt for her was duty, a reality that sent prickles of anguish to her heart. She didn't want Derek

Colton's protection. She wanted…well, she didn't know *what* he wanted, but it wasn't that.

The sound of the front door opening had Sawyer shooting to his feet. "Derek's back," he said with a grin, tearing out the door.

Chloe smiled ruefully. Lord, was there *anyone* who didn't think Derek had hung the stars and moon?

She heard the two Coltons chatting in the front hall, then Derek's deep voice saying, "Back to the main house, Squirt. Julia says you didn't finish your homework." There was an annoyed groan, some more muffled words and then Sawyer shouted, "Bye, Amelia!" and the door opened and shut again.

A moment later, Derek appeared in the doorway. His navy blue sweater stretched over his big shoulders, his defined pecs flexing as he crossed his arms over the wide expanse of his chest. "I spoke to Felix," he said without preamble.

Chloe slowly rose from her chair. "And?"

"And I have no idea what to think. He didn't give any overt signs that he knew who I was, but he did say a couple of things that made me question what he knew."

"Like what?"

"At one point he referred to you in the present tense—"

"What?" she interrupted as horror slammed into her.

Derek bridged the distance between them and placed his hands on her waist to pull her closer. "It could've been a slipup. A lot of folks continue to talk about those they've lost using the present tense."

"Did he say anything else?"

"He got a little intense and started grilling me about whether I was dating anyone."

Panic rippled through her. "Oh, God. See? He knows about us!"

"I have no clue what he knows," Derek said with a sigh.

She blew out a frustrated breath. "We have to assume he knows everything. He's punishing me, Derek. He probably decided to amuse himself by sending me the wedding stuff while he consulted on that case, and now that the surgery is over, he's going to make his move."

Derek's shoulders stiffened. "I won't let that bastard within two feet of you, Chloe."

She sighed. "I have to face him sooner or later."

"No, you don't." He practically glared at her. "The divorce and restraining order can be handled through lawyers and cops. You're not going near Felix ever again, sweetheart. I don't care if I have to throw you over my shoulder and lock you in my bedroom—you're not going near him."

She had to laugh. "Wow. I kind of like this caveman Derek. Are you going to thump on your chest a couple of times, too?"

"No. But I wasn't kidding about the throwing you over my shoulder part."

The next thing she knew, he scooped her into his arms and settled her in a fireman's carry. As she alternated between laughing and protesting, he marched out of the kitchen and carried her into his bedroom, where he deposited her on the bed.

She landed with a bounce, laughing harder when Derek actually thumped his chest, grinning widely at her. Then the humor in his eyes faded, replaced by a smoldering flash of seduction. "Do you realize I haven't seen you naked all day?" he rasped.

The giggle that slipped out of her mouth was *so* not suited for a woman her age. "I hadn't noticed," she said impishly.

"I think we need to change that." He got on the bed next to her, his warm hands traveling under the hem of her shirt to stroke her suddenly feverish skin.

Before he could pull the shirt over her head, Chloe stilled his hand and met his eyes. "What are we doing here, Derek?"

His long silence confirmed that he knew she was referring to more than this simple, playful exchange. "Enjoying each other's company," he finally said.

She couldn't help the rush of disappointment. That was it?

With a sigh, she rose on one elbow and studied his handsome face. "How do you feel about me?"

The unease in his expression cut her to the core. "I..." He trailed off.

"Are we...are you..." Another breath left her mouth, followed by a string of questions she couldn't rein in. "Why are you doing so much for me? Why did you see Felix today? What's going on between us?"

"I care about you," he said gruffly.

Okay. Well, that was a start.

"And I'd do this for anyone," he added.

She felt as if someone had dumped a bucket of icy water over her head.

Derek hurried on, completely oblivious to her state of distress. "You're in trouble, and I want to help. Because I care."

Because he's the ultimate protector, a bitter voice corrected.

Chloe battled the hot sting of tears, blinking rapidly before he noticed how quickly she was unraveling beside him. Pasting on a smile, she disentangled herself from his embrace and slid off the bed.

"Where you going?"

"Bathroom," she said in a light tone.

From the corner of her eye, she saw his shoulders relax, but relaxed was the last thing she felt as she headed for the washroom.

I'd do this for anyone.

She shut the door behind her and approached the mirror, feeling like a total fool as she examined her weary reflection. Of course he'd do it for anyone. Derek Colton rescued people. He helped them, supported them, cared for them.

And she was just another one of the people he took responsibility for. Like the downtrodden patients he'd found work for on the ranch. The Double C's housekeeper, Margie, Jimmy the ranch hand, even his siblings' nanny was someone who'd been down on her luck before Derek swooped in to save the day.

It shouldn't surprise her that she was no different, that Derek considered it his duty to save his new nurse from her abusive husband.

But it still disappointed her. Big-time. Especially because her feelings for Derek had nothing to do with duty.

Chloe twisted the faucet and bent down to splash water on her face. The water was cold, but it was the wake-up call she needed, a frigid reminder that her involvement with Derek had gotten too serious. The intimacy of the situation was too confusing, too misleading, which indicated that it was time to put the brakes on this romantic relationship with Derek before she completely lost her head.

And her heart.

Chapter 11

The next morning, Derek found Chloe at the kitchen table, huddled in front of his laptop. A steaming mug of coffee sat next to her, along with a plate of gooey cinnamon buns that made his mouth water. Ever since she'd moved in, he'd been waking up to the aroma of freshly baked treats or delicious breakfasts, and damned if he couldn't get used to that.

The domesticity of the situation disturbed him, however, as did the head-scratching conversation they'd had last night. He knew he must be sending her mixed signals, making love to her every night yet unable to put a label on their relationship, but he had no idea how to deal with the emotions plaguing him. Familiar emotions. Unfamiliar ones. Having a woman's presence in his home again reminded him so much of being married to Tess, but at the same time, Chloe was nothing like his late wife. Whereas Tess had brought desperation and chaos into his life, Chloe brought warmth. She soothed his soul—and that scared the hell out of him.

"What are you doing?" he asked as he entered the kitchen, eyeing her curiously.

"Checking for flights," she replied without looking up.

Every muscle in his body tensed. "Why?"

"I want to book a flight to L.A., preferably for tonight or tomorrow."

His heart sank to the pit of his stomach, joining the knot of panic already forming there. "Why so soon?"

"I figured I could meet with a lawyer while Felix is in Philly 'consulting' on his case. Then when he returns to the west coast in a few days, I'll have some ammunition to use when I officially reveal I'm alive."

Derek clenched his teeth so hard his jaw throbbed. Chloe still hadn't met his eyes, and he could tell from her rigid shoulders that she was upset. But why? What had changed from last night to this morning? Why was she rushing to go back to the west coast?

"I know you said you'd come with me," she went on, continuing to avert her eyes. "But I won't hold you to that, Derek. In fact, I think it's better if I handled this alone."

"I disagree," he said coolly.

With a sigh, she finally made eye contact. "Then you're still planning on coming to California with me?"

He met her weary gaze with a pointed look. "Yes."

After a beat, she sighed again. "All right. I guess I'll book two flights, then."

Derek squared his shoulders. "Don't book anything yet."

She wrinkled her forehead.

"I want to look at our appointment calendar first and see what I'll need to juggle around. In fact," he said hastily, "maybe I'll do that now."

As he edged toward the door, Chloe glanced at him in surprise. "Like right now?" she said, agape.

He nodded fervently. "Yeah, right now sounds good. I'll drive over to the clinic and take a quick look at the calendar." He halted in the doorway. "Set the alarm once I leave, and don't go anywhere. I'll be back soon."

Without waiting for a reply, he darted out of the kitchen, knowing Chloe was probably confused as hell by his sudden departure. He didn't blame her—he was feeling pretty confused himself as he donned his coat and boots and hurried out of the house.

What are you doing, man?

He ignored the internal inquiry and got into his car. The thought of Chloe getting on a plane—without him—had him clenching his fingers over the steering wheel. No way would he let her go to California alone.

Scratch that—no way would he let her go to California *at all*. She'd already admitted that Eden Falls felt like home to her, and there was no reason for her to return to the west coast. She could file for divorce and get a restraining order here.

Flicking on the window defroster, Derek didn't wait for the car to warm up before starting the engine and speeding away from the ranch. He tapped his fingers on the steering wheel as he followed the road leading toward the interstate. He had no intention of going to the clinic to check a damn calendar. As far as he was concerned, Chloe wouldn't be boarding any westbound planes in the near future. She wouldn't have to— because Derek was going to make sure Felix Moreno didn't bother Chloe ever again.

Derek knew that Moreno was supposed to meet Burt Winters at nine to sign some papers, and Derek planned on intercepting the man before he left the hospital. If it came down to it, he was willing to use violence to get his point across. Moreno might be a world-famous plastic surgeon, but Derek had four years of college football on his side, not to mention that two-year stint on Penn State's wrestling team.

He had no qualms about knocking the bastard off his high horse and making it clear that Chloe was off-limits. Now that he'd concluded his consultation, Moreno didn't have any reason to remain in town, and Derek was determined to send him packing.

And if he doesn't know she's alive?

The thought made him falter. If Moreno truly was in the

dark about Chloe, then Derek would pretty much be announcing to the man that his wife wasn't dead.

Then again, that was something Chloe planned to do, anyway. Moreno would find out the truth the second Chloe filed for divorce, so at this point, what did it matter who Moreno heard that truth from?

Thirty minutes later, Derek reached the hospital and pulled into the parking lot. Just as he was about to kill the engine, his peripheral vision snagged on a familiar figure.

Moreno.

The surgeon was crossing the lot, a cell phone glued to his ear as he made his way toward a sleek silver Lexus.

Derek immediately slid lower in his seat and ducked his head so Moreno wouldn't spot him, but the precaution was unnecessary; the surgeon was focused on his phone call. Making an angry gesture, Moreno clicked the electronic remote in his hand and the Lexus honked in response. A second later, Moreno slid into the driver's seat and an engine roared to life.

Derek was in the process of debating whether or not to follow Chloe's husband when the Lexus suddenly sped out of the lot in a squeal of tires. Huh. Where was Moreno going in such a hurry?

Curiosity getting the best of him, Derek reached for the gearshift and stepped on the gas. On the main road, Moreno's car slowed to a more reasonable speed, prompting Derek to stay a few cars back. He'd never tailed anyone before, but Moreno didn't seem to notice he was being pursued. His car threaded through the streets of downtown Philly, making its way west.

Derek felt more exposed once they entered an industrial area without much traffic, leaving him directly behind the Lexus. Beads of sweat popped on his forehead. He nearly pulled a U-turn, giving up on this foolish chase, but before he could, the Lexus's taillights blinked red and Moreno slowed in front of a strip of warehouses that had seen better days.

A frown puckered his lips. What the hell was Moreno doing

here? The buildings on this stretch of road looked abandoned, most of them boasting chained-up doors, sagging roofs and graffiti-covered walls. When the Lexus made a right turn into a gravel parking lot, Derek continued going straight, but he kept his gaze glued to the rearview mirror.

Moreno had parked the car in front of a one-story warehouse with a sloped roof and steel doors. Derek slowed down, watching in the mirror as Chloe's husband hopped out of the car and darted toward the entrance of the building.

The moment the man disappeared through the doors, Derek executed a U-turn. He didn't use the lot where the Lexus sat but drove to the one across the street instead. He parked the car, then bounded out of the vehicle, adrenaline spiking in his blood as he made his way to the warehouse on the other side of the road.

He approached the steel doors with caution, prepared for Moreno to burst out at any second and demand to know why Derek was following him. But when he neared the double doors, one of which was ajar, he heard Moreno's muffled voice drifting out of the interior of the building. The surgeon was still on the phone.

Sucking in a calming breath, Derek stepped closer and risked a peek through the open crack of the door. All he saw was darkness, but he heard footsteps, along with Moreno's voice, which grew more and more agitated. Snippets of sentences met his ears, most of which made absolutely no sense.

"As sterile as it's going to be… Are you sure the medical staff you hired is competent?"

Derek frowned. What the hell was the man talking about?

Moreno's angry voice boomed from the interior of the warehouse. "I'm putting *my* butt on the line here!" A pause. "That's *exactly* what I'm saying…Your men are reckless and stupid… I don't care if the Amish bitch tried to escape…"

A chill went through Derek's body. *What?*

"Your idiot goons need to control themselves! I'm not risk-

ing my butt and my career to fix your mistakes, you understand? This is a one-time deal only. Next time one of your
men gets out of hand, call another surgeon." Moreno let out a
stream of muffled curses. "Bring her at six o'clock. The staff
and I will prep this place…Yeah…won't take more than a few
hours, depending on the damage."

The call sounded like it was winding down. Releasing the
stunned breath he'd been holding, Derek bolted away from the
building and hurried back to his car. Shock and apprehension
warred inside him, and the ice slithering through his veins refused to dissipate.

I don't care if the Amish bitch tried to escape.

His fingers shook as he shoved the key in the ignition and
started the car. Shooting one last look at the warehouse, he
stepped on the gas and peeled out of the lot, reaching for the
cell phone he'd left in the cup holder. He dialed Tate's number,
put the phone on speaker and waited for his brother to answer.

"Colton," came the brisk voice.

"Tate, it's me. Where are you?"

"At my apartment. Why? What's up?"

Derek didn't bother with explanations. "I'm on my way
over."

Suspicion laced Tate's voice. "What's going on, Doc?"

"Just stay put." His jaw tensed. "I'll explain everything
when I get there."

"Are you sure?" Tate demanded twenty minutes later, looking as stunned as Derek felt.

The two Coltons stood in Tate's living room in front of the
large picture window overlooking downtown Philly. Derek
had just relayed the conversation he'd overheard, still unable
to fathom how any of this could possibly be true.

Unless there was another explanation for what Derek had
heard, Felix Moreno was somehow involved in the disappearance of those Amish girls.

"That's what he said," Derek confirmed, a sick feeling settling in his stomach.

Tate's light blue eyes hardened with resolve. "Moreno said an Amish girl tried to escape?"

He nodded. "And it sounded like one of the men who was supposed to be watching her lost control. Moreno is definitely performing some kind of surgery tonight, Tate. The girl will be brought to the warehouse at six."

"Jesus."

"So what now? Will you put a team together to storm the place?"

"I'll try," Tate said grimly. "But I don't know if my supervisor will go for it."

"Why the hell not?"

"Because the only evidence we have that anything shady is going down is a one-sided conversation you overheard. I can't lead a commando raid on private property without a warrant. Without going through red tape." Tate made a frustrated sound. "Wait here. I'm calling Villanueva."

As Tate marched toward the kitchen, Derek shifted his gaze back to the window, watching the late-morning crowds scurrying along the sidewalks below. His brain still reeled as the implications surrounding Moreno's conversation coursed through it. How could Moreno be connected to the missing Amish girls? Law enforcement had linked the disappearances to an online sex ring—why would a renowned plastic surgeon be involved with something like that? And how long had Felix been a potential player in the ring? Was it a recent business venture for Moreno or a longtime arrangement?

Derek's mind continued to spin as Tate strode back into the room, his stiff shoulders revealing that his supervisor hadn't told Tate what he'd wanted to hear. "Villanueva says I can't go in without a search warrant."

"Then get a warrant," Derek shot back.

"He's gonna try, but he doesn't think a judge will sign off

on it. There's no proof that what you heard has anything to do with this case. In fact, there's no proof anything sinister is going down at all. No just cause."

Frustration simmered in his gut. "What about an arrest warrant for Moreno?"

"Villanueva is hesitant to get one, especially because, again, there's no evidence of any illegal behavior. Moreno is a public figure, and if we're wrong about this, the bastard could put the department through lawsuits and unwanted media attention."

Derek shook his head in disbelief. "So you're just going to let him perform some illegal surgery on an innocent girl tonight?"

Tate's expression was surprisingly calm. "Of course not."

His spine went rigid as he stared at his brother. "You're going alone," he accused.

"Damn right I am."

Derek sighed. "Then I'm coming with you."

"No way," Tate said immediately. "You're a civilian, Derek. I'm not involving you in this. Besides, I'm liable to get in real shit for this. Villanueva will can my ass if this goes south."

"Well, he can't fire me." Derek crossed his arms over his chest. "I might be a civilian, but I'm also a doctor. If Moreno is operating on a patient tonight, you might need me, Tate. Who knows what he'll do to that girl?"

Tate hesitated.

"You need me," Derek said firmly. "And I'm not letting you do this alone. I'm going with you, bro."

After a moment, Tate caved. "Fine. But we do it my way. If I say jump, you jump. Understand?"

"Yes, sir." He had an afterthought. "Should we bring Emma in on this?"

Tate's features hardened. "No."

"Why not? I thought the department was working with the Feds on this case."

"We are, but…" Tate's voice went hoarse. "We don't know who the girl is, Doc. I don't want Emma there, in case…"

It dawned on him then. "In case the girl is Hannah Troyer," he finished quietly.

Derek understood Tate's reluctance to involve Emma. Hannah was the younger sister of the man Emma loved. Who knew what condition they would find Moreno's patient in? If the girl *was* Hannah, Emma would be the one to break the news to Caleb Troyer.

"It can only be you and me," Tate said in a tone that invited no argument. "For all we know, you could've misunderstood Moreno's side of the phone call. This mysterious surgery of his might not have to do with the case."

"Yeah, it might have something to do with Chloe," Derek said harshly.

Tate hesitated. "What's going on with that, anyway?"

"Nothing really." Ill at ease, Derek drifted toward the kitchen, hoping his brother wouldn't follow him.

But Tate stayed right on his heels, his blue eyes burning a hole in Derek's back.

In the kitchen, Derek slid onto one of the tall stools at the eat-in counter, while Tate leaned against the fridge, continuing to study him with suspicion. "What do you mean, 'nothing really'?"

"She's still staying at the ranch."

"And?"

"And she's decided to file for divorce and get a restraining order against Moreno." He gritted his teeth. "She's determined to go back to California to straighten everything out."

"You don't sound too happy about that."

"I don't want her anywhere near that psycho," Derek snapped. "She can straighten things out here. She doesn't need to put her life at risk by facing that man."

Tate let out a soft whistle. "Wow."

"Wow what?"

"You're really protective of her. Like more protective than usual."

Derek shrugged, focusing his gaze on the ceramic bowl of apples on the granite counter. "Your fruit is starting to rot," he remarked. "You should toss it."

"And you should know better than to change the subject." Tate leaned forward, resting his elbows on the counter. "You're sleeping with her, aren't you?"

"That's none of your business, Tate."

"I'll take that as a yes." His brother cocked his head. "Are you in love with her?"

Panic streaked through him. "Of course not."

"Why do you say it like that? Would it be so bad, being in love with her?" Tate asked quietly.

He swallowed. "Chloe is a wonderful woman, okay? She's smart, kind, beautiful. And I…I respect her."

"That's it? You *respect* her?"

"I like her," he amended. "I like her, respect her, desire her, but love? That's not what this is about."

"Then what *is* it about?"

Derek faltered. Damn it. He didn't want to talk about his feelings for Chloe. Not when he himself didn't even understand them.

"I don't know," he finally said.

Tate must have decided to take pity on him because he dropped the subject. "Are you sticking around here until we go?"

Shaking his head, Derek slid off the stool. "No, I want to head back to the ranch and talk to Chloe first. She was trying to book a flight to L.A. earlier, and I'm not convinced I managed to talk her out of it. I want to make sure she stays put until we investigate this warehouse thing tonight. If Felix is involved with those missing girls, I don't want Chloe confronting him just yet."

His brother shrugged. "And if he is involved, she might not have to confront him at all."

"What do you mean?"

"He'll be in jail and out of her hair." Tate shot him a pointed look. "And then she'll be free to be with you."

Derek's answering silence had Tate sighing again.

"Look," Tate said roughly, "I don't know Chloe very well, but I saw the way she looked at you when she came over for dinner and again when I stopped by your place the other night. The woman cares about you, Doc. She cares a lot."

Derek swallowed.

"And you know I'm not one to dish out love advice, but clearly you need to hear this. Women don't like to guess what the man in their bed is feeling. So if you love Chloe, tell her." Tate's expression went somber. "If you're not honest with her, Derek, you're only going to lose her in the end."

When Derek walked through the front door a couple of hours later, Chloe instantly knew something was up. His face was grave as he said, "We need to talk."

Of course. She'd been expecting this ever since he'd hurried out of the kitchen earlier as if he were being chased by a wild dog. She knew her decision to go back to California had upset him, but Chloe didn't know what else to do. She couldn't stay at the ranch any longer. Derek's inability to tell her how he felt about her or what he wanted out of their relationship told her more than she wanted to know.

As he led her into the living room and gestured for her to sit, a feeling of foreboding rose up her spine. His sober expression and unblinking eyes hinted that more was at stake here than the uncertain status of their relationship.

"What's going on?" she demanded as she settled on the couch.

"You can't leave the ranch."

She frowned. "We already talked about this. I'm going to California—"

He cut her off. "This isn't about California or the divorce or anything we talked about this morning. This is serious, sweetheart. You need to stay at the ranch, at least for one more night."

"Why? What's happening?"

"I followed your husband today."

She gave a sharp intake of breath. "What? Why?"

"I wanted to confront him," he said roughly.

Her eyes widened. "I told you not to do that!"

"I know, but I wasn't going to let you go back to L.A. I planned on taking care of it, but things got…complicated."

"What does that mean? What the hell is going on, Derek?"

With a deep exhale, he told her.

Chloe's pulse raced as his words registered in her brain. "*Felix* might be involved in the disappearance of those girls?"

"It sure as hell sounded that way."

Wave after wave of shock slammed into her. Her head spun like a merry-go-round, making it difficult to focus on any one thought. Her husband was a potential player in a *sex ring*. How was that even possible?

If it were true, then that meant Chloe had never really known her husband at all.

"Wait a minute," she burst out, suddenly grasping one of the details Derek had sprinkled in during his explanation. "You and Tate are going after him *alone?*" Disbelief flooded her belly. "That's insane! You need to involve the police."

"Tate can't get a warrant to search the warehouse. So we're going to investigate on our own and call for backup depending on what we find."

"Fine. Then I'm coming with you."

Derek blanched. "No way."

She shot to her feet, angrily bearing down on him. "Yes way. If what you're saying is true, and Felix is performing a surgery, then you'll need another medical professional on hand. Who knows what shape the girl will be in?"

His features strained. "This is too dangerous for you."

She glared at him. "But it's not dangerous for *you?*"

"Chloe—"

"I'm going with you," she interrupted. "You might need my help with the patient."

Something flashed in his eyes. It took Chloe a second to realize that what she saw in those gorgeous brown depths was not anger but awe.

Her cheeks heated. "Why are you looking at me like that?"

His eyes shone brighter as he took a step toward her. Lifting a hand to her cheek, he ran his fingertips along her skin. "I'm looking at you because I've never met a woman as strong as you."

He shook his head in amazement. "You constantly surprise me, Chloe. The way you jumped in and helped me tend to Violet's injuries last month. How you opened your heart to Sawyer even though he reminds you of everything you've lost. Your determination to raid a warehouse tonight just in case a patient might need your help." His fingers traced the seam of her lips. "Tell me, sweetheart, how could you ever consider yourself weak?"

Surprise and pleasure mingled in her blood. "Maybe I just need to start seeing myself through your eyes."

When Derek leaned in to kiss her, she couldn't find the willpower to resist. His lips brushed hers in a fleeting caress, evoking the familiar rush of heat, the sensation of pure and utter belonging that Derek instilled in her.

Breaking the kiss, Chloe touched his cheek and smiled. "Thank you for seeing the strength in me."

His voice came out gruff. "You're welcome, sweetheart. Now, about tonight—"

Her expression hardened. "I'm coming with you," she reiterated. "If that kiss was meant to distract me or make me forget about your plans, it didn't work, *sweetheart.*"

His lips twitched in humor.

"I'm serious, Derek. If Felix is hurting those girls, I'm going to help you stop him."

This entire "operation" was a bad idea.

As Tate glanced at his two passengers, he wondered how the hell he'd gotten roped into bringing along not only one civilian, but two. Nevertheless, he had to give Chloe Moreno credit—she refused to back down, even when Tate had threatened to throw her in the trunk of the car if she didn't go back to the ranch.

In the end, she'd agreed to wait in the car while he and Derek investigated the warehouse, although not before she'd weaseled a promise out of Tate that if her medical skills were needed, he'd call her in.

Tate had parked the sedan across the street from the warehouse, behind an oversize Dumpster that ensured they remain out of sight. From his vantage point, he spotted three cars in the gravel lot on the other side of the road, including Felix Moreno's Lexus. There were no windows on the north-facing exterior of the building, but a pale glow spilled from under the front doors, indicating activity on the inside.

Reaching into the glove compartment, Tate handed Derek a nine-millimeter Beretta. Although Derek was the only Colton who'd chosen a career that didn't involve a gun, Tate knew his brother had a permit to carry.

"Remember how to use this?" Tate asked briskly.

Derek rolled his eyes. "You think I can ever forget all those times you and Gunnar dragged me to the shooting range?"

"It's a precaution," Tate reminded him. "Don't use it unless you absolutely have to."

"Damn. I was hoping to go on a shooting spree."

"Was that a joke, Doc?"

"He's been doing that a lot lately," Chloe piped up from the backseat. "I know, right? I didn't think he was capable of humor, either."

Tate hid a smile. He suspected Derek's mellowing had everything to do with the woman who'd just spoken, but he kept his thoughts to himself. He didn't understand why his brother couldn't admit that he had real feelings for the pretty blonde, but Tate was confident Derek would smarten up soon. He usually did.

All traces of humor died as he cast another look at the warehouse. Dread circled his gut like a school of sharks. What would they find beyond those doors? *Who* would they find?

"All right, let's do this," Tate said in a low voice. He glanced over his shoulder. "Stay in the car, Chloe, and don't get out unless Derek or I call. You've got your cell?"

She held up her phone, her expression all business.

"Good." With a nod, he slid out of the driver's seat, then adjusted the shoulder holster containing his weapon.

He and Derek both wore black shirts, trousers and boots. They had no coats, but Tate barely felt the chill in the air as they cut across the street toward the warehouse. Earlier in the day, he'd managed to get his hands on the blueprints for the building, thanks to a far-too-trusting clerk at the city's zoning office. He'd discerned that there were two ways in: the double doors out front and a door in the rear. The back entrance involved a series of hallways that eventually led to the main space of the warehouse; Tate figured it was their best option in terms of catching anyone off guard.

"Stay behind me," he ordered.

He and Derek crept alongside the chain-link fence bordering the side of the building, making their way to the back. A minute later, Tate let out a soft curse when he discovered the rear door was boarded shut.

"Front door it is," Derek murmured.

They rounded the building, staying close to the wall as they neared the entrance. Not a single guard manned the double doors; obviously Moreno and his people didn't feel they needed any protection. Unless the bulk of their man and firepower waited beyond those doors, Tate thought uneasily.

Tate signaled for Derek to watch his back, then ducked through the front doors, praying they wouldn't creak. Fortunately, his entrance was soundless, and he didn't encounter a solitary soul as he stepped into the warehouse. A single lightbulb dangled from a string above the entryway; its glow revealed paint-chipped walls and a floor covered with dust and wood splinters. The building used to house a woodshop, according to Tate's research.

He stepped deeper into the cavernous space, Derek hot on his heels. Both men drew their weapons when murmured voices wafted out of a hallway to the left.

Exchanging a look with his brother, Tate slunk toward the source of activity. The voices grew louder, words becoming less muffled and more terrifying.

"She's under."

"Vitals?"

"BP, one-twenty over eighty."

"Jesus, look at what that animal did to her..."

Tate felt queasy. Unwittingly, the image of Hannah Troyer's beautiful face flashed across his brain. He'd never been a religious man, but in that moment he couldn't help but utter a silent prayer.

Please, God, don't let it be her.

Standing flat against the wall, he peered into the corridor. Crap. A bulky man clad in camo pants and a bomber jacket stood guard in front of one of the doorways in the hall, a sleek black Glock in his hand.

Tate ducked out of sight. "Guard at the door," he said in a barely audible voice. "Need to take him out."

"How?" Derek whispered.

He set his jaw, his gaze scanning the floor. When he spotted a splintered piece of what looked like a chair leg, Tate bent down and picked it up. Taking a breath, he threw the piece of wood at an aluminum ladder leaning against the wall a few yards away.

Derek jumped as the ladder toppled over with a deafening crash. "What the—"

A second later, the guard burst out of the corridor. Just as he turned the corner, Tate came up behind the beefy man, clapped a hand over his mouth and slammed the butt of his gun into the back of the man's head.

Unconscious, the guard dropped to the floor like a sack of potatoes.

"Nice," Derek murmured, looking impressed.

Tate offered a small grin, which faded the moment he made his way to the doorway the guard had been covering.

"Vitals are stable," came a crisp female voice.

Inhaling, Tate opened the door and peered into the room.

And nearly keeled over in shock.

He felt like he was watching a macabre episode of some medical television drama. An impromptu operating room had been set up in the high-ceilinged space. Overhead surgical lights illuminated a large operating table surrounded by stainless-steel tables bearing surgical instruments, an anesthesia cart and various blinking monitors.

Three people occupied the room, all wearing lime-green scrubs, white surgical masks and booties on their feet. One sat near the patient's head, the anesthesiologist, Tate deduced. The other two hovered over the table, talking in hushed whispers. Moreno and his nurse.

"Retractor," the surgeon barked.

The female next to him placed an instrument in his gloved hand.

Tate's heart dropped to the pit of his stomach as he watched Moreno lean forward. The silver instrument he held gleamed in the overhead lights, flickering like a mirror in the sun as he lowered his hand to his patient's face.

The patient.

Tate couldn't see the patient.

Wait…there. Moreno shifted, revealing a still figure lying on the table. Her face was red and swollen, unrecognizable. A white plastic cap covered her hair.

Tate's mouth went dry. God, what color was her hair? Hannah had such beautiful red hair. What color was the girl's hair, damn it?

"Scalpel," Felix ordered.

As the nurse placed a silver blade in Moreno's open palm, Tate snapped out of his panic-induced trance and sprang into action.

Charging toward the table, he raised his gun and yelled, "Philadelphia Police Department! Put your hands in the air!"

A shocked silence fell. The only sound in the room came from the monitor next to the table, a sharp, steady beeping indicating the patient's heartbeat.

And then chaos broke out.

"Oh, God!" the nurse shrieked.

The anesthesiologist jumped off his chair and tried to make a run for it, only to halt like a deer in headlights when Derek raised his own weapon and shouted, "Don't move!"

The man froze.

"Step away from the table!" Tate snapped at Moreno.

He rushed forward, keeping his gun aimed at the surgeon and nurse and leaving Derek to handle the remaining man.

Thanks to the mask he wore, Tate could only see Moreno's eyes, those dark pupils that suddenly flashed with fury.

"You're making a big mistake," Moreno roared. "I'm conducting surgery, for God's sake!"

"In a warehouse?" Tate said, his voice dripping with disbelief. Without awaiting a reply, he waved his gun at the surgeon. "Step away from the table, Moreno. Now."

Those dark eyes warily shifted from Tate's face to the barrel of his Beretta. After a long beat, Moreno moved away from the patient.

"Stand against the wall, hands on your heads. All of you," Tate ordered, indicating with his gun where he wanted them to go.

The trio shuffled toward the wall, Moreno cursing up a blue streak every step of the way.

Reaching into his pocket, Tate fished out his cell phone and tossed it to Derek. "Speed dial two. Tell Villanueva I need backup ASAP."

Derek caught the phone and started dialing.

Tate went for his pocket again, pulling out the FlexiCuffs he'd shoved in there. As he restrained Moreno's hands behind his back, the surgeon twitched with outrage.

"I'll have your badge for this!" Moreno spat out.

"You're in no position to make threats," Tate replied coolly.

"Villanueva's sending a team," Derek called. "I'm going to check on the patient."

Tate secured the plastic cuffs around the wrists of Moreno's nurse, then did the same to the anesthesiologist. As he ordered the trio to get on their knees, he saw from the corner of his eye Derek rushing to the operating table. The gasp that followed made Tate's blood run cold.

"Do you recognize her?" Tate's throat tightened. "Is it Hannah?"

"I can't tell," Derek yelled. "But damn it, Tate, she needs to be in a hospital."

Unable to turn his back on his prisoners, Tate was forced to listen to Derek's indecipherable mumbling. "Fracture of the zygomatic bone...swelling in the nasal region... Jesus, Tate, her cheekbone's collapsed into the maxillary sinus."

"English, Doc," Tate said in frustration. "What's wrong with her?"

"Broken nose, fractured cheekbone, more facial trauma

I can't assess." The beeping from the monitor maintained a steady rhythm, but Derek's tone was urgent as he said, "I need you in here."

It took Tate a second to realize Derek hadn't spoken to him but into the phone. He must have called Chloe.

"You're making a dire mistake," Moreno muttered from his spot on the floor. "Your interference could very well cost my patient her life."

"Shut up," Tate snarled. "I don't think you understand how much trouble you're in, *Doctor.*"

His mocking tone set Moreno's eyes ablaze. "You have no idea who I am, do you, *Detective?* I'm Felix Moreno. I've got more money than you'd ever know what to do with and I can squash your pathetic little career with one phone call. You have no *idea* what you walked in on, the kind of trouble you'll be in once the people in charge find out—"

Moreno halted midsentence, a wheezy breath bursting out of his mouth.

Tate heard the footsteps from behind, turning in time to see Chloe skid into the room carrying Derek's black medical bag.

Moreno's dark eyes widened as they focused on the woman in the doorway. Looking like he'd just seen a ghost, he whispered, *"Chloe?"*

Chapter 12

Chloe stayed rooted to the ground. Ten feet away, her husband crouched on his knees with his arms behind his back. Green scrubs clung to his large, muscular body and a surgical mask dangled around his neck. A chill snaked up her spine when she caught sight of his familiar face, those chiseled, angular features, the cleft in his square chin, the flawless olive skin and familiar dark eyes—eyes that were wide with sheer disbelief.

On the other side of the room, Derek stood by an operating table that seemed unbelievably out of place in this cold, damp room. His brown eyes sought her out, but she shifted her gaze back to Felix, her palms tingling.

Her first instinct was to cower, to crawl inside herself the way she always did when faced with Felix's rage. Instead, she reined in the impulse and forced herself to walk toward him, her head high.

"Hello, Felix," she said coolly.

His jaw opened and closed. "Chloe. You're...*alive.*"

The shock hanging on each word didn't fool her. This sick bastard had been toying with her for more than a week now. Sending the blood-soaked dress. The DVD. The cake. He'd known the wedding keepsakes would drive her mad with terror, had probably laughed about it, patted himself on the back for his successful torment of his wife.

"Drop the act," she snapped. "We both know this isn't a surprise to you."

His dark eyes sizzled with fury. "Don't speak to me in that tone, you little bitch!" He staggered forward as if to charge at her, but the sharp wave of Tate's gun made him freeze. He focused on Chloe, that perfect face of his hardening. "You faked your death?"

"You already knew that," she said bitterly. "Isn't that why you've been sending me all those delightful presents?"

He shook his head. Over and over. As if truly bewildered. But Chloe didn't buy the pretense, not one damn bit.

"I *mourned* you!" he growled. "And this entire time, you were alive? Hiding from me? *Laughing* at me behind my back?"

He looked so insulted she had to laugh, which only triggered another explosion. "I won't let you get away with this, you hear me? You're going to pay for this, Chloe."

"Give it up, Felix, you can't hurt me anymore."

"I can do whatever I want! I'm your *husband*," he roared. "And I'll damn well punish my wife for her betrayal!"

Chloe's gaze drifted to the unconscious girl lying on the operating table. Derek was monitoring her vitals, but Chloe knew he was listening to every word being said.

"You're sick," she whispered, shifting her gaze back to Felix. "So much sicker than I ever knew."

Felix laughed, long and slow. "You're the sick one, Chloe. Defective. Weak. Pathetic."

The pang of sorrow she experienced was no match for the rivaling jolt of fury that spiraled through her. "I am not weak," she said quietly. "I managed to escape you, didn't I?"

His eyes narrowed.

"That's right," she continued. "I escaped you, Felix. I'm free now." Now *she* laughed, gesturing to his cuffs. "Too bad you can't say the same."

As if on cue, the doors of the warehouse burst open and a team of law enforcement officials streamed in. Brusque shouts bounced off the walls, and footsteps thudded on the floor. Paramedics rolled in a gurney, hurrying toward Derek and the patient, their voices urgent as they assessed the situation.

Derek stepped aside to give the emergency workers room to work. His brown eyes locked with Chloe's, and in that moment, she didn't care that he couldn't admit his feelings for her. Didn't care that they'd probably say goodbye.

No, the only thing she cared about was getting away from the despicable man she'd married and being with the man she loved.

As she took a backward step, her husband snarled. "Don't walk away from me." When she kept walking, his voice became even more enraged. "I'm your husband! You can't walk away from me, Chloe!"

"Watch me," she murmured.

She walked straight into Derek's arms. They embraced briefly, his strong hands caressing the small of her back. Then they turned to watch the scene before them.

As Felix was carted off, he continued shooting incensed looks over his shoulder, scowling at Chloe. Halfway to the door, the scowl became a smile. A fat, smug smile that sent a shiver of fear straight to her bones.

"This isn't over!" Felix called out. "Don't forget who I am, Chloe. I have money, power—you really think I'll go to jail for trying to save an innocent girl's life? I'll be back, Chloe! I'll be back and you better be ready to—"

His voice faded as the cops hauled him out of the warehouse.

Chloe stared at the door for a long time before turning to watch the paramedics wheel the patient away. She winced when she glimpsed the girl's face—red and purple, swollen to the size of a melon, completely unrecognizable. They'd take her to the hospital, where she'd undergo surgery in a real O.R. with a surgeon who wasn't a psychopath. Thank God.

Next to her, Derek remained oddly silent.

"Are you okay?" she asked.

"I should be asking you that," he said gruffly.

A uniformed officer holding a radio stalked in their direction. "I'm going to need you to leave the scene, folks," he barked. "Forensics needs to do a sweep."

Taking her hand, Derek led her out of the warehouse, keeping one arm around her trembling shoulders. Chloe couldn't believe everything that had happened. Seeing Felix again. Watching him being carted off in handcuffs.

And his final, *Terminator*-esque threat continued to haunt her mind.

I'll be back, Chloe.

Fear coated her throat, but she breathed through it. No, Felix would not follow through on his threats. He was going to jail.

Outside, the sun had already set, the parking lot bathed in darkness. Cruisers with lights flashing and unmarked vehicles were parked on the gravel. Derek's brother stood near a police van, in deep discussion with two of the officers who'd arrived on the scene.

Beside her, Derek stayed quiet, a frown now marring his mouth.

Chloe studied his face. "What's bothering you?" she asked uneasily.

His cheeks hollowed as if he were grinding his molars.

"Seriously, what's wrong?" She clutched his hand. "It's over, Derek. Felix will go to jail for his part in…in whatever the hell went down tonight. He can't hurt me anymore."

"I don't know, sweetheart. I'm not convinced he was behind those twisted gifts." He shook his head, visibly upset. "He seemed genuinely shocked to see you alive."

"He's a damn good liar," she said curtly.

Doubt continued to flicker in his eyes, but before he could respond, Tate strode over to them, a hard but victorious expression on his face.

"You can take my car back to the ranch," he said. "I'm heading to the hospital with one of the uniforms." Then Tate

miled and extended his fist. "Thanks for being my partner
n crime, Doc."

Derek bumped knuckles with his brother. "Anytime, De-
ective." He suddenly sobered. "Any idea who that girl is?"

"Not Hannah Troyer or Mary Yoder, judging by the hair
olor," Tate replied, sounding relieved. "And I caught a glimpse
f her arm as she was being wheeled out—she has a large birth-
mark, just like one of the missing girls from Ohio. I'll have
o check the case file to be sure." He swallowed. "We'll run a
DNA sample because we can't identify her face, but the good
news is, she'll live."

Chloe thought about that girl's battered face and flinched.
She couldn't believe Felix had been involved in those disappearances. She still didn't understand his part in it, but after
onight, she had no doubt that her husband had been sicker and
hadier than she'd ever imagined.

Tate dropped by early the next afternoon, just as Chloe and
Derek had settled in the kitchen for a cup of coffee. They'd
spent most of the day marveling over last night's shocking de-
velopments, and Derek had been checking periodically with
he hospital for updates on the Amish girl's condition.

She'd been identified as Miriam Schwartz, a seventeen-year-
old girl who'd been reported missing from an Amish community in Ohio two months ago. Miriam would undergo several
more plastic surgeries to correct the damage to her face, and
she'd yet to regain consciousness after this morning's surgery.
The police and the Feds hoped that once she came to, she'd be
able to provide them with information about her captors and
wo-month-long ordeal.

"Thanks," Tate said, accepting the coffee Derek handed
him. He joined them at the table and wrapped his fingers
around the mug. "So, I spent the morning interrogating your
husband, Chloe."

The amazed look in Tate's light blue eyes brought a wry smile to her lips. "He's a real piece of work, huh?" she said.

"I don't think I've ever met a more arrogant human being," Tate answered. "He truly believes he'll walk away scot-free from all this."

Dread climbed up her throat. "But he won't, will he?"

"No way in hell. Even if he cuts a deal, which he's trying to do, he'll end up serving substantial jail time. Most of the missing girls are underage, some as young as fourteen, and our justice system takes crimes against children very seriously."

"I still don't understand what Moreno's part in all this was," Derek spoke up with a frown.

"I can shed some light on that." Tate rolled his eyes. "Moreno's been singing like a canary all morning in the belief that if he sells out his cohorts, he'll save himself. Five months ago, he heard about this potentially profitable business investment. He was doing a consultation in New York at the time, and a mutual friend put him in contact with the ringleader of this sex ring."

Derek's breath hitched. "Wait, Moreno's met the ringleader?"

"Not quite. They only communicated over the phone. All Moreno knows is that the man lives in Manhattan." Tate took a quick sip of coffee. "Anyway, Moreno liked the idea of fattening up his wallet—"

Chloe barked out a humorless laugh. "Of course he did. The only thing he loves more than power is money."

"He also poured some of his own cash into the 'project' to help get it off the ground," Tate explained. "He was promised a cut of the profits and was assured that the girls involved were in high demand."

She shook her head, battling equal parts confusion and disgust. "Amish girls are in high demand?"

"Apparently so." Tate looked equally disgusted. "Sweet, innocent, pure as the driven snow. Perverts can't wait to get their hands on these girls and indulge in their darkest fantasies."

"And Felix helped kidnap them?" Chloe said in dismay.

"From what he says, he was just an investor, but he also flew out to perform a couple of surgeries and provide medical assistance when needed." Tate grimaced. "He claims that the girls are drugged during their captivity because it's easier to transport them to the buyers that way. One girl had a bad reaction to the drugs and Moreno was called in to treat her. But other than the occasional medical emergency, Felix was really just reaping the profits from the venture."

Chloe was horrified. She couldn't believe her husband was involved in something so despicable, yet a part of her wasn't surprised to hear it. Felix Moreno was a sociopath, a psychopath and a power-hungry narcissist with a God complex. Knowing him, he'd gotten off from the thought of powerless girls at the mercy of sick, wealthy men.

Anger bubbled in her stomach as she pictured Felix counting his big stash of money, turning the other cheek while innocent girls—*children*—were being victimized and sold like cattle in the sex trade.

"So what now?" she asked tightly.

"Now we charge your husband with every damn count we can make stick, and the bastard goes to prison."

"In that case, you should question him about Jim Maloney." She fought a wave of sadness. "Jim was a friend of mine in L.A."

"Chloe believes Felix killed him," Derek said quietly.

"Contact Detective Patty Burgess at the LAPD," Chloe suggested. "She was in charge of the investigation, so she'll know more. But there's no doubt in my mind that Felix had my friend killed, Tate."

Derek's brother nodded. "I'll do that. Thanks."

"Did Felix confess to breaking into Chloe's apartment and leaving those gifts?" Derek spoke up.

"No, he continues to deny it. But he's not convincing anyone of his innocence, considering…"

"Considering what?" Derek asked sharply.

Tate hesitated. "He's made several death threats against Chloe already, which is another reason the prosecutor is going to argue against bail during the bail hearing."

Chloe's breath caught, but before she could say anything, Tate's cell phone rang.

He brought it to his ear and answered with a quick "Colton."

While Tate took the call, Derek reached out and squeezed Chloe's hand. "I won't let Felix hurt you," he murmured. "His threats mean nothing."

She swallowed, wanting very badly to believe that.

Across the table, Tate's handsome face took on a hard edge. "I'll be right there," he barked into the phone, then hung up.

"Everything okay?" Derek asked.

Taking a last sip of coffee, Tate got to his feet. "That was Villanueva. Our informant came through on a location. I'm going in tonight."

Chloe frowned. "Going in where?"

"Tate is posing as a buyer," Derek said grimly. "He's allowed to inspect the girls before he 'buys' one."

She gasped. "Are you serious?"

"As a heart attack," Tate confirmed. He took a step to the door. "I'll keep you guys posted if I can."

After Tate left, Chloe gripped her coffee cup, unable to comprehend everything she'd just heard. "I can't believe I was married to that man for twelve years," she mumbled. "Clearly I never knew a damn thing about Felix."

Derek reached across the table to squeeze her hand. "Moreno is an accomplished liar. He fooled a lot of people."

"I guess." She hesitated for a beat but couldn't stop her next words from spilling out. "Knowing the kind of man he really is makes me all the more grateful that I have someone like you in my life now."

She didn't miss the way Derek shifted in discomfort.

Releasing a resigned breath, she met his deep brown eyes nd said, "What's going on here, Derek?"

Derek knew exactly what Chloe was asking him, yet he ill felt the need to stall. "What do you mean?" he asked, laying dumb.

She sighed. "You know what I mean, Derek. What happens ow? With us?"

"Now you file for divorce, just like you were planning to do. nd you can stay in Eden Falls, just like you wanted."

"And?"

He fidgeted with his hands. "And what?"

"I'll keep working at the clinic with you?"

"Of course."

"And the rest of it? You and me, sleeping together…?"

"I was hoping we could keep doing that, too."

She smiled faintly, but it faded fast. "Are we in a relation- ip, Derek?"

He gulped. "Sure."

Another sigh slipped out of her throat. "Wow. That sounded incredibly enthusiastic."

Derek stifled a frustrated groan. He knew he'd hurt her ith that lackluster declaration, but this sudden interrogation ade him nervous. He had to wonder—what *did* he want from hloe? Now that Felix was out of the picture, she was free. his strong, beautiful woman was his for the taking—all he ad to do was reach out and grab her.

So why couldn't he seem to take that final step? Look into er hazel eyes, open his mouth and tell her how he felt about er?

"I get it," she said when his silence dragged on too long. he staggered off the chair and carried their empty mugs to e sink. Then she headed for the door.

"Where are you going?" he asked, battling a spark of alarm.

"To pack my things."

Derek was on his feet in an instant, sprinting after her. H
noticed the rigid set of her shoulders, the stiffness of her leg
as she marched toward the bedroom.

Choking down a lump of panic, he caught up to her in th
hall, latched his hand onto her arm and met her sorrow-fille
eyes. "You don't have to go, Chloe."

"Yes, I do." Her lips tightened. "Now that Felix is gone
there's no reason for me to stay here. I don't need your pro
tection any longer, and you can play the savior for someon
else now."

Derek bristled.

She raised a brow. "What? I'm wrong? I'm not just the lat
est person you felt the need to save?"

What?

"No," he retorted, frustration seizing his throat. "It's mor
than that and you know it."

"I don't know anything," she shot back. "That's the problem
Derek! You haven't once told me how you feel about me." He
tone softened. "I know it's hard for you. But do you think it
easy for me? We both had really crappy marriages. We bot
have some serious baggage. But the time we've spent togethe
has taught me so much."

He was floored by the sheer emotion on her face.

"I realized that not all men are like Felix. You showed m
that some men are gentle. Loving. You helped me recover m
own strength." She let out a breath. "I want more than a pro
fessional relationship with you. I want more than sex. I…I'
in love with you, Derek."

Derek felt like someone had punched him in the gut. Shoc
pleasure and distress clamored for his attention.

"I need to know how you feel about me," Chloe said softly
"I need to know that this thing between us is about more tha
you rescuing me the way you rescue everyone else."

Derek's palms went damp. He wanted so desperately to te

er he felt the same way, but something stopped the words from leaving his mouth.

His silence stretched on for much longer than he'd intended, prompting Chloe to shake her head in disappointment. "I need to pack. I'll move back into my apartment this evening."

She spun on her heel, moving toward the bedroom.

"Chloe, wait."

She stopped, slowly turning to face him again.

"Don't go," he said hoarsely.

"Why not?" When he didn't answer, she crossed her arms. "Give me a reason to stay."

Drawing a deep breath, Derek opened his mouth—only to be interrupted by his ringing cell phone.

"I have to get this," he said hoarsely. "I'm on call."

Resignation flickered in her eyes. "I know."

Ignoring the deep ache in his heart, Derek answered the phone and heard the frantic voice of Burt Watson, the husband of one of his patients. "Doc, you've gotta come quick!" Burt's loud exclamation nearly shattered Derek's eardrum. "Cindy went into premature labor!"

"Have you called an ambulance?" Derek inquired briskly.

"Yeah, but I don't think they'll make it in time. It happened so fast! One second her water broke, the next, she started pushing. I can see the head, Doc. You need to get here *now*. Jesus, I can't do this alone."

"I'm on my way." Disconnecting the call, Derek turned to Chloe, his brain snapping into professional mode.

"I have to go," he said without delay, already marching down the corridor. He shot a quick glance over his shoulder. "Don't go, Chloe."

"Derek—"

"Please," he pleaded, "can you just wait until I get back so we can finish this?"

She nodded, but as he hightailed it out of the house, he could have sworn he heard her murmur, "But it's already finished."

* * *

Chloe spent the next half hour packing her stuff, knowing without needing to talk to Derek that it was time to leave his house. She'd move back to her apartment in town, but how long she'd stay there, she didn't know.

God, she longed to stay in Eden Falls. To spend her days working with Derek and her nights in bed with him. But if he couldn't admit how he felt about her, then what was the point? She'd already spent twelve years with one emotionally unavailable man and she didn't need another one.

She carted her duffel bag to the front hall, her legs feeling like they were made of lead. She kept picturing the devastated look on Derek's face when she'd announced that she was leaving. Deep down, she knew he cared about her. Perhaps he even loved her. Or hell, maybe he didn't. Maybe he truly wasn't over his wife's death and never would be.

Either way, she didn't want to play guess-what-Derek's-feeling anymore.

When the cordless phone on the hall credenza began to ring Chloe was eager for a respite from her unhappy thoughts. She grabbed the phone as if it was a life preserver and she was drowning at sea. "Hello?" she blurted out.

An unfamiliar female voice greeted her. "Amelia?"

Chloe frowned. "Yes…"

"This is Dr. Greenleigh from Philly General."

She relaxed. "Dr. Greenleigh, hi."

"I spoke to Dr. Colton and he asked me to give you a call and relay the news I just gave him. He couldn't call himself because he was on the way to the hospital with a patient, but he said you'd want to know this sooner rather than later."

Chloe wrinkled her forehead. "Okay."

"The Danford results came in. Rachel signed a form allowing me to release the results to Dr. Colton and yourself." The oncologist paused. "The mass we removed from Rachel's breast was a fibroadenoma, which as you probably know is benign. I'm recommending against removal due to its small size and because it isn't causing her any discomfort, but we'll keep monitoring it."

Relief shuddered through her. "That's wonderful news."

"Yes. Dr. Colton said you'd be happy to hear that. So was I. In my field, I'll take all the good news I can get."

Chloe was smiling as she hung up the phone. Rachel and Jacob would be thrilled by the news, and she made a mental note to pay a visit to the couple's farm when she had a chance. For a second she considered calling, then rolled her eyes to herself as she remembered the Amish couple didn't have a phone. Besides, a visit would be nice. Seeing a happily married couple might boost her spirits.

She sighed, feeling like a total fool and more than a little embarrassed as she thought about that awkward conversation with Derek. She'd told the man she'd *loved* him, and he'd just stood there, wide-eyed and mute.

The sigh transformed into a groan. Okay, she needed to get out of this house. She fully planned on keeping her promise to Derek and sticking around until they finished their "discussion," but she decided some fresh air might do her some good. Maybe she'd take a drive in the meantime, attempt to clear her head before Derek returned from the hospital.

On the porch, she hesitated, remembering Derek's insistence that she not go anywhere alone. But now that Felix was in police custody, what did she really have to fear? Felix couldn't hurt her anymore.

No, only Derek could do that now, if he continued to keep her at a distance.

Putting on her gloves, Chloe descended the porch steps, her boots crunching in the thin layer of snow covering the front yard. She slid into her Toyota and started the engine, and as she waited for the car to warm up, she wondered where to go.

A visit to town might be nice. She could window shop, maybe find some holiday gifts for Sawyer and Piper. And

Derek, though she had no clue what present she could possibly buy him. She'd already given him her heart, and he'd run away like a frightened animal.

As heat blasted out of the car's vents, Chloe drove away from the ranch and headed for the main road. She flicked the radio on, but the crooning country ballad that floated from the speakers only depressed her further. Shutting off the music, she welcomed the silence, focusing on the road ahead.

At the last minute, she decided to keep driving right through Main Street toward the outskirts of town, realizing she had no desire to be around other people. No, what she wanted was peace and quiet.

It was pure, unconscious instinct that brought her to Eden Falls Bridge. She followed the river, then pulled onto the road shoulder and parked in the same place she had the last time she'd been here. Hopping out of the car, she gazed at the snow-covered trees to her left. If she strained her ears, she could hear the muffled rush of water from Eden Falls. Her safe place. The place where Derek had shown her the sensual side he'd been hiding since the day they'd met. The place where the barriers between them had come crashing down.

She took a step toward the snowy slope, then stopped, her hand sliding into her pocket to grab her cell phone. She suddenly realized that she'd neglected to leave a note for Derek telling him where she was going. Knowing he'd worry if he came home and found her gone, she dialed his number, deciding a call was in order.

She got his voicemail, as she'd figured she would.

"Hey, it's me," she said after the automated prompt. "If I'm not at the house when you get back, don't freak out. I went for a drive. I needed a quiet place to think. Oh, and Dr. Greenleigh called with the news about Rachel's biopsy. Thanks for having her notify me."

The purr of an engine caught her attention. Chloe turned

rowning when she noticed a black SUV with tinted windows lowing down as it approached.

"Uh, sorry, lost my train of thought," she muttered into the phone. "Anyway, I'll be home soon and…" To her shock, the UV came to a stop directly behind her car. "So yeah, I'll talk o you when…"

The SUV's driver door opened.

Chloe gasped. "Oh, God."

The cell phone fell from her hands and clattered onto the vet slush at her feet.

Her jaw went slack, eyes widening as she watched Bianca Moreno striding toward her.

No, that couldn't be Bianca. Those were someone else's cat-ike green eyes, someone else's dark curly hair and designer oat.

Someone else's face-lift? a voice taunted.

Chloe stared at the familiar Botox'd mouth, the plasticlike live skin and unnatural tightness of flesh. She blinked rapidly, vondering if she'd officially gone off the deep end. Clearly this vas a figment of her imagination. A hallucination. It *had* to be.

But then the figment of Chloe's imagination opened her nouth, which was pulled as tight as Chloe remembered. "Hello, larling. It's been far too long, hasn't it, Chloe?"

She gaped at her mother-in-law. Before she could even try o make sense of Bianca's presence here, the woman lifted one nanicured hand, revealing the small silver pistol in her grasp.

With a smirk, Bianca raised the gun and gestured at the rees. "Start walking."

Chapter 13

Chloe couldn't contain her shock as she stumbled through the woods. The barrel of Bianca's gun dug into her back, and the one time she'd tried looking over her shoulder to stare at the woman, she'd been rewarded by a sharp jab in the tailbone.

A low-lying branch scraped Chloe's cheek and stung her flesh, making her wince. Her breath came out in white puffs, her feet aching inside the high-heeled leather boots that were not meant for a trek through the forest. And the entire time she walked, her bewilderment remained at an all-time high. What the *hell* was Bianca doing here? Had Felix phoned his mother from jail and informed her that his wife was still alive?

This isn't over.

Felix's menacing words buzzed in the forefront of her brain. Was Bianca exacting Felix's revenge for him?

She sucked in a deep breath, ducking to avoid another low branch. "Bianca," she started.

"Shut up," her mother-in-law snapped. "You don't get to talk until I say you can. Now keep walking."

Chloe kept walking.

Several minutes later, they neared the waterfall, but she didn't feel an ounce of the serenity she'd experienced when she'd come here with Derek. She staggered onto the rocky bank, scanning the ground at her feet for anything she could use as a weapon. That jagged rock the size of a grapefruit had potential, but the long stick near the pool at the base of the waterfall looked even more promising.

Chloe edged toward it, only to halt when Bianca said, "Don't move."

That throaty voice shouldn't belong to a woman in her seventies. Hell, that *face* didn't belong to a woman in her seventies. Bianca Moreno had had no qualms about using her son's expertise to combat her own aging process. She looked twenty-five years younger than she was, her statuesque form oozing wealth and status.

Twigs crackled, and then Bianca appeared, her pistol aimed at Chloe's forehead. The older woman didn't speak, just slanted her head and appraised Chloe, those shrewd eyes sweeping up and down, side to side.

She swallowed. "How did you find me? Did Felix call you?"

"Felix? Heavens, no. I saw your whore face in a tabloid magazine," Bianca answered with a derisive snort. "Imagine my surprise, seeing my daughter-in-law right there in the pages of my gossip rag, tending to an injured actress when she's supposed to be *dead*."

Chloe furrowed her brows. Tabloid magazine? Injured actress? The only actress she'd had contact with since faking her death was Violet Chastain, but how—

The answer flew into her head like a gust of wind. After Violet's attack, Chloe had been wheeling the actress out of Derek's clinic. Tate and Emma had warned them there might be photographers hanging around, and clearly one had snapped their picture that day.

And since Bianca read every celebrity and beauty magazine ever published, it was no wonder she'd come across the photograph. Bianca was obsessed with appearances; Chloe had frequently witnessed the woman marking up pictures of starlets' faces and ordering Felix to do the same thing to her.

As understanding dawned, Chloe met Bianca's gaze. "Wait a minute. *You're* the one who was sending me those presents?"

Bianca rolled her eyes. "Who else would it be, darling?"

Oh, God. Bianca. Not Felix. Derek's doubts hadn't been un
founded, after all. Felix's shock over seeing her at the ware
house had truly been genuine. He hadn't known Chloe was
alive.

"But…why?" She shook her head. "Why torture me? And
why the hell are you holding a gun to me now?"

"You actually have to ask why? You ruined my son's life!"
Bianca replied harshly. "You hooked him into marriage and
made his life miserable."

"Me?" Outrage slammed into her. "Your *son* was the one
who *beat me.* Your *son* was the one who *scarred me!*" She ges
tured wildly at her face, despite the makeup covering the scar

Bianca just laughed. "You deserved that, you stupid whore
Flirting with other men in front of your husband? What kind
of self-respecting woman does that?"

Chloe gawked at her mother-in-law. Did the woman actu
ally believe her own words? From the molten rage burning in
those green eyes, clearly she *did* believe it. Lord, the woman
was out of her mind. Utterly certifiable.

Bianca's hand trembled as she glared at Chloe, but on her
face not a single muscle moved. Too many cosmetic proce
dures had frozen those facial muscles, leaving Bianca with
only a handful of expressions, anger and distaste being her
most prominent ones.

"So what now? You're going to kill me?" Chloe asked
warily eyeing the gun in Bianca's hand.

"Killing you is the only way to get you out of my son's life."

A laugh flew out of Chloe's mouth. "I was already out of
his life! Jesus, Bianca, I *faked my death*." Chloe's laughter got
louder, a stitch forming in her side. "You got what you wanted
you idiot! I was gone."

"And you would've come crawling back," Bianca spat out
"You're pathetic, Chloe. Weak. You need my son. You can't live
without him. The moment I realized you were alive, I knew

had to take care of you once and for all. I stayed out of it during your wretched marriage—"

She snorted at the bald-faced lie.

"—and I kept my mouth shut because my son asked me to. He was under your spell, but the spell was finally broken when you died. Felix and I had never been closer," Bianca revealed in a haughty voice.

Chloe wanted to gag. "You're sick, Bianca."

"And you're pathetic. I knew you'd come back eventually, begging him to take you back."

"So you decided to send me a bunch of sick presents to scare me?"

"To watch you squirm," Bianca corrected. "But I got bored of that. Now, I just want you gone. You're never going to bother Felix again. You won't get anywhere near him."

She laughed again. "Neither will you, seeing as he's in jail."

"What did you say?"

Chloe shot her a pointed stare, but Bianca's blank expression didn't change. A startled breath left Chloe's mouth as it dawned on her. "You don't know, do you?"

"Know what?" her mother-in-law asked suspiciously.

"Felix is in jail, Bianca. Your perfect, precious son is in *jail*."

Derek exited Philadelphia General with a bittersweet smile on his face. He'd just left Clara and Burt Watson with their tiny baby girl cradled in the new mom's arms. Five pounds, six ounces. A month premature but healthy and beautiful and already the apple of her parents' eyes.

As happy as he was for the couple, seeing the newborn had reminded Derek of the baby he'd lost, the one Tess had taken from him when she'd driven their car over that bridge.

It ate at his insides that he'd never definitively know why Tess had died. If she'd known about their baby when the car sailed over the bridge. If she'd hit the water by accident or with the knowledge that she was finally putting herself out of her own misery.

But one thing Derek *did* know—Chloe would never have done that to him.

He knew it with the utmost certainty, with not a shred of doubt in his mind. Chloe had fought hard for her babies, desperate to keep them, devastated to lose them. And no matter how many times Felix knocked her down during their marriage, she'd stumbled back to her feet. She hadn't let the depression consume her the way Tess had. No, Chloe had battled her demons and come out swinging.

Derek froze in his tracks as the realization truly sunk in.

Chloe wasn't Tess. She would *never* be Tess.

And another eye-opener was that he'd spent the past two years thinking that *he'd* disappointed *Tess,* but it had been the other way around. Tess had disappointed *him.* She'd taken the love he'd offered and thrown it back in his face.

The same way he'd done to Chloe earlier.

Shame constricted his heart. She'd told him she loved him, and what had he done? Stared at her like an idiot, then said they'd finish the conversation later.

What the hell was the matter with him?

As he strode across the parking lot, Derek whipped out his phone, needing to hear Chloe's voice. Needing to assure her that he was on his way back and finally, finally ready to talk about how he felt.

When he flipped open the phone, he discovered that Chloe had beat him to it. The missed call display revealed her cell number, and a message icon flashed on the screen.

Derek dialed his voicemail and punched in the pass code.

A second later, Chloe's voice filled the line.

"Hey, it's me. If I'm not at the house when you get back, don't freak out. I went for a drive. I needed a quiet place to think."

Unlocking the driver's door of his car, he listened to the

rest of the message with half an ear. Chloe's voice took on a distracted note, but it wasn't until she gasped that Derek grew worried. He heard her say "Oh, God" and then a clatter filled the line, as if she'd dropped the phone.

His back stiffened with worry, which only intensified when he heard a husky, unfamiliar voice, a woman's voice, mingled with the sound of footsteps and the soft hiss of the wind. When he made out the words "Start walking" he sprung to action.

Panic slicing into his gut, he started the engine and peeled out of the visitor's parking lot.

Chloe was in danger. He knew it with a certainty that cut right to the bone.

His foot shook on the gas pedal as he sped away from the hospital. It would take him thirty minutes to get back to town, half that time if he ignored the speed limit and took the toll route instead of the interstate.

Focusing on driving proved difficult; fear and dread coursed through his blood.

I'll be back, Chloe.

Moreno's parting words buzzed through Derek's brain, making him wonder if he'd been wrong to believe the shock he'd seen on Moreno's face when the man had laid eyes on Chloe.

Had Moreno been responsible for the sick presents all along? Had he arranged for a third party to take care of Chloe in the event that he couldn't?

Or had the threats come from someone else the entire time—this mysterious woman, perhaps?

Too many questions raced through his mind, and his hands began to shake as he reached for his cell phone again. He wanted to call Tate, or Emma, or hell, a damn SWAT team. But what would he say? He had no idea where Chloe even was.

I needed a quiet place to think.

She'd mentioned a drive, so that meant she had her car, but where would Chloe have gone? As anxiety clamped around his throat, Derek scanned his brain, trying to remember if Chloe had any favorite places in town. He'd only ever seen her at the clinic or her apartment. Neither would offer a place to think.

The waterfall.

Derek let out a ragged breath. Of course. Her safe place. She would've gone to her safe place to think.

His heartbeat quickened as he whizzed along the highway, going double the speed limit and not giving a damn. Ten minutes later, he burst off the exit ramp, nearly skidding into a ditch as he tried to maintain control of the car.

When he neared Eden Falls Bridge, he didn't even experience that usual burst of heartache. For the first time in two years, he wasn't thinking about Tess as he crossed the bridge. He was focused solely on Chloe, and his chest squeezed with panic at the thought of what he might be walking into.

Nothing good, he realized grimly, when he spotted Chloe's car, along with an unfamiliar black SUV, parked on the side of the road.

Battling a jolt of terror, Derek stopped the car, then snapped his phone to his ear and dialed Emma's number.

"What's up, Doc?" came his sister's amused voice.

He ignored the teasing remark. "Emma, I need you to call the sheriff. Tell him to get to Eden Falls right away. The waterfall, I mean." His voice came out in sharp pants. "Tell him to come to the waterfall. Chloe's in trouble."

"What kind of trouble?"

Derek stumbled out of the car. "I don't know, Em. I'd call Tate but he already left for New York. I have no idea what I'm walking into and I need backup, so call the sheriff *now.*"

He hung up before she could respond, rounding the vehicle to unlock the trunk, where he'd stashed the gun Tate had given him last night. He'd planned on giving it back to Tate earlier, but it had slipped his mind, and now he was grateful for the oversight. Popping the trunk, he grabbed the weapon and shoved it in the pocket of his coat. Then, jaw tight with resolve, he hurried down the slope toward the tree line.

She's okay. It'll be okay.

He clung to the assurances echoing in his mind, but no matter how hard he tried, he couldn't fight the terrifying feeling that he was too late.

"No," he muttered to himself, anger swamping his gut.

It wasn't too late. He refused to believe the universe hated him so much that it would take Chloe from him the way it had taken Tess.

With quick, determined strides, Derek followed the riverbank toward the waterfall. Snow and twigs were crushed beneath his boots, the rhythmic cracking noises matching the fast thump of his heartbeat. When the faint sound of rushing water greeted his ears, he slowed his pace, ducking to the left so he could approach the waterfall from the trees rather than the muddy bank.

"You're a goddamn liar!"

He froze as the enraged voice cut through the cold afternoon air.

Creeping through the brush, Derek neared the base of the falls. Through the trees two figures entered his line of sight. He made out Chloe's blond hair. A flash of red—Chloe's scarf.

He moved closer, then eased behind the thick, gnarled trunk of a towering pine tree and peeked around it. His muscles tensed as he stared at the back view of the woman facing Chloe. Dark curly hair, a long gray coat flapping in the chilled breeze.

And then Chloe's soft voice drifted in his direction. "It's true. Your son was helping to kidnap Amish girls and selling them to sex predators."

Your son.

Christ. This was Bianca Moreno, Felix's mother.

Derek had a tough time keeping his jaw closed as he absorbed the startling revelation.

"You're lying! My Felix would never involve himself in something like that," Bianca hissed.

The voices grew murmured again. Derek swallowed hard,

then continued his approach, ducking behind another tall pine just as a maniacal laugh bounced off the trees.

"This time there won't be anything fake about your death," the tall woman said mockingly.

Derek glimpsed a gleam of silver. His heart dropped to the pit of his stomach when he realized Moreno's mother held a pistol in her hands. Oh, Jesus. Chloe had told him her mother-in-law was a tyrant, but clearly the woman was also insane.

"You're going to commit suicide," Bianca announced.

Derek tightened his grip on his gun. From his vantage point he saw the blood drain from Chloe's face. He heard Bianca Moreno as she said, "And this time you're going to succeed, darling."

"You're crazy," Chloe burst out.

"And you're pathetic," the woman snapped.

Derek crept closer, lifting his weapon. A twig snapped beneath his boots. He froze, his body tensing, but Bianca didn't whirl around.

Chloe, however, must have heard the noise because her gaze shifted in his direction.

Shock flooded her hazel eyes. As her mouth fell open, Derek shook his head and shot her an urgent look, then lifted his free hand to his mouth and pressed a finger to his lips.

Chloe's jaw swiftly closed.

Adrenaline pulsated in his blood. He glanced at the back of Bianca Moreno's head, then at Chloe again. Taking a breath, he held up three fingers, then pointed down to the ground, hoping Chloe understood the message he was trying to transmit.

When she gave an imperceptible nod, he nodded back, his face hard with fortitude.

"I think you're going to shoot yourself in the heart," Bianca decided, taking a step closer. "The temple is more in line with suicide, but the note you'll leave will mention a broken heart. A long, heartfelt message to your new lover, saying you still love your husband and can't bear to lead him on any longer. I feel that's poetic, no?"

Derek held up one finger.

Bianca took a step toward Chloe.

He raised a second finger, then a third.

Chloe dropped to the cold ground like a stone.

A second later, Derek sprang on Bianca and tackled the woman to the ground. An outraged wail echoed in the air, followed by a clatter and a wet *plop* as the pistol in the woman's hand fell into the pool of water beyond the rock-strewn bank.

With a grunt, Derek straddled Bianca Moreno's back, jamming a knee between her shoulder blades as the woman wiggled and screamed beneath him. While he attempted to subdue the squirming, infuriated woman, he sent a quick glance in Chloe's direction. "You all right, sweetheart?"

Looking dazed, Chloe staggered to her feet. "I'm good."

Beneath him, Bianca continued to struggle, thrusting her elbow back and nearly connecting with his groin. Derek shifted and grabbed hold of Bianca's dark curls. "Don't move," he growled.

The woman shrieked when he yanked on her hair. "Let go of me, you bastard!"

He rammed the butt of his gun into the nape of her neck. "Don't make me shoot you," he said in a weary voice.

At the threat, she immediately went still.

Chloe stumbled over, looming over Derek and Bianca, a stunned, slightly exhausted expression on her pretty face. "I can't believe you found me," she murmured, her eyes meeting his. "How did you know I was here?"

"You said you needed a quiet place to think." He swallowed. "Somehow I knew this is where you'd go."

"Colton!" a loud voice shouted. "Colton, you down there?"

"Over here," Derek called.

Footsteps crunched in the snow, and then three men lumbered onto the scene, weapons drawn. Two wore the beige uniform of the Eden Falls Police Department, whereas the third, a man with wavy brown hair and shrewd green eyes, was clad in jeans and a heavy parka; Derek instantly recognized Tom Hanson, the lone detective who worked for the department.

The next ten minutes went by in a blur. Derek and Chloe quickly explained to Hanson and his men what had transpired, while Bianca cursed and screamed the entire time, hurling threats at anyone she could. When one of the officers fished her pistol out of the water, the woman denied it was hers. When Hanson slapped handcuffs on her bony wrists, she shrieked in indignation. When she was read her rights, she nearly head-butted the detective.

By the time Bianca was ushered away, her delusional, un-balanced nature was clear to all. As Bianca and the cops dis-appeared, Derek heard Bianca demanding to see her son, screaming out Felix's name over and over again.

Stunned, he turned to Chloe, whose hazel eyes flickered with sorrow.

"You okay?" Derek asked gruffly.

Chloe tore her gaze from Bianca's retreating figure. "I…" Her voice cracked. "Thank you," she finally whispered. "You saved my life."

Without an ounce of hesitation, Derek drew her into his arms and held her so tight he feared he'd crack her ribs. Loosening his grip, he buried his nose in her hair and breathed her in, letting her sweet scent infuse his senses. He couldn't believe he'd almost lost her.

When he felt moisture soaking his neck, he realized Chloe was crying. "It's over, sweetheart," he murmured. "Neither of them can hurt you ever again."

She sniffled, then lifted her head and gazed up at him. "Thanks to you."

A short silence settled between them, during which Derek took a deep breath and collected his composure. "I have to tell you something," he said roughly.

She nodded, and from the disillusioned expression on her face, he realized she was expecting the worst. Expecting him to tell her he didn't want to be with her.

Not wanting to put her through even another second of pain and uncertainty, he said, "I love you, Chloe."

Her jaw fell open. "What?"

"I couldn't say it before," he mumbled, wincing in shame. "I was too much of a coward. But I mean it, sweetheart. From the moment you walked into my life, something changed. I was closed off for so long, blaming myself for Tess's death, but today I realized that it wasn't entirely my fault."

She searched his face. "What do you mean?"

"Maybe I *did* fail Tess, but you know what? She failed me, too. She refused to heal herself, choosing to play the part of the victim rather than try to fix anything. And her death wasn't my fault. Tess was mentally ill—nothing I could have done would have saved her." Residual fear trickled through him. "When I saw Bianca pointing that gun at you, I almost died, Chloe. The thought of losing you…"

"You saved my life, Derek." She looked achingly beautiful and unbelievably timid as she gazed into his eyes. "But I need to know that's not the only reason you're saying any of this. I don't want to be rescued. I just want to be loved."

As emotion clogged his throat, Derek leaned in and brushed his lips over hers. "Can't I do both?"

She smiled through her tears. "Yes, I suppose you can."

Derek couldn't keep his hands off Chloe on the drive back to the ranch. He held her hand. Leaned over to stroke her cheek. Sneaked a kiss when they stopped at a stop sign. His heart had damn near stopped when he'd seen Felix Moreno's crazy mother wielding a gun at Chloe. In that moment, he'd known without a doubt that he didn't want Chloe to leave. Eden Falls, *or* him.

Now, with Chloe cuddled up next to him in the passenger seat, Derek had never felt more content.

"I can't believe both Bianca *and* Felix are facing jail time," Chloe murmured.

He squeezed her hand. "Like mother, like son?" he said in a feeble attempt at humor.

But that earned him a genuine laugh. "I guess so. Apparently I married into a crazy family."

Derek stopped at the entrance of the Double C, then hopped out to open the gate. A second later, he slid back in the car and steered in the direction of his house. Shooting Chloe a sidelong look, he noted the smile curving her lips. "What are you thinking about now?" he teased.

"I was thinking how happy I was to be home." She sounded slightly awed. "Which made me wonder when I started to consider this ranch home."

That's because it is *your home,* he nearly said, but bit back the words at the last second. They'd yet to discuss where their relationship was heading now, and he didn't want to pressure her into moving in with him on a permanent basis. As much as he wanted her to.

And it looked like any decisions about their future would have to wait. Derek suppressed a groan as he spotted Emma, Sawyer and Piper waiting on his porch, but when he registered the genuine worry creasing their faces, he realized he'd neglected to call Emma and tell her what happened at the waterfall.

No wonder his siblings looked ready to kill him when he and Chloe stepped out of the car.

"What happened?" Emma demanded, bounding toward them with Sawyer and Piper on her heels. She turned to Chloe with a look of concern. "Chloe, are you okay?"

"Chloe?" Piper wrinkled her brow. "Who's Chloe? I thought Amelia was missing."

Clutching Chloe's hand, Derek shot his younger sister a rueful smile. "I think we've got some explaining to do." He turned to Emma. "Moreno's mother was the one sending Chloe all those presents." His throat went tight. "She tried to kill her."

"But Derek got there just in time," Chloe said softly.

Sawyer glanced from one to the other. "I am seriously confused," the boy announced.

Sighing, Chloe approached Sawyer. "I've been lying to you, Squirt. To everyone, in fact."

He frowned. "Go on…"

Derek hid a smile.

"My name isn't Amelia. It's Chloe." She hastily gave him the short version of the story, omitting the more personal details involving the abuse and miscarriages.

When she finished, both Sawyer and Piper gaped at her. "You're married?" Piper gasped.

"You crashed a plane into the ocean?" Sawyer breathed.

The contrasting tidbits each kid had taken from the story made Derek laugh.

"Soon to be divorced," Chloe told Piper in a firm voice. "And yes," she said to Sawyer.

This time, Sawyer seemed more intrigued by her first comment. "Wait—if you're getting divorced, does that mean you're going to marry Derek?"

She faltered. "Um…"

Sawyer frowned again, then turned to his brother. "Dude. You didn't ask her?"

Derek grinned. "I was too busy saving her life, Squirt. Cut me some slack."

Sawyer raised his eyebrows. "Well, you don't look busy now."

Derek glanced at Chloe, who didn't look the least bit put off by where this discussion had gone. In fact, she just grinned and said, "He's got a point, Doc."

His lips twitched. "Well, I guess you've twisted my arm."

Her eyes widened as he sank to his knees in front of her. "Derek! I was kidding! You don't have to—"

"I don't have to do anything," he agreed, reaching for both her hands.

His three siblings gawked at him as if he'd sprouted horns and a tail. Of course they'd be surprised, he realized. He was Derek Colton, after all, the least spontaneous man on the planet.

But Chloe had brought out a side he never knew he had. Making love to her in front of a waterfall in the dead of winter. Having sex in his office. Going caveman on her and carting her off to his bedroom. She brought out his playful side and not only that, she made him happier than he'd felt in years.

"I love you," he said huskily, tilting his head to meet her beautiful hazel eyes. "I love your big heart. I love your strength. I love your intelligence. I love every last thing about you. And I will never hurt you, Chloe. I promise you that."

"I know," she whispered.

"What I will do is love and honor you," he said through the lump in his throat. "And I'll save you whenever you need saving, sweetheart. Not because I'm a natural-born protector, but because I owe you."

She shot him a quizzical look. "What do you mean?"

"You saved me," he said simply. "You brought me back to life, Chloe. I raised a shield around my heart, and you knocked it right down. You showed me that it *is* possible to love again." He stroked the centers of her palms. "Let's start fresh together, sweetheart. Marry me."

"Yes."

There was no delay on her part. In fact, she spoke so fast he felt inclined to search her face. "Are you sure?"

Smiling, she slid down to her own knees and cupped his jaw in her hands. "I've never been more sure of anything in my life. I love you, Derek, and I want nothing more than to be your wife."

Joy soared through him, spurring him to yank her into his

arms and kiss her. So long and deep that he totally forgot they had an audience until he heard Emma clearing her throat.

He and Chloe pulled back sheepishly to find his siblings watching them. Piper in wonder. Emma with approval. And Sawyer in total disgust.

"Dude," his little brother grumbled, "that was embarrassing. The lovey-dovey speech and the smooching? Ugh. I'm *never* gonna get all moony over a girl." He glanced at Chloe, then his sisters. "No offense."

"None taken," they said in unison.

Derek helped Chloe to her feet and wrapped an arm around her, then glanced at Sawyer with knowing eyes. "Talk to me in a few years," he said wisely. "When it comes to girls, I bet you'll be the biggest sucker of us all."

"Never!"

Rolling her eyes, Emma clapped a hand over Sawyer's shoulder. "Come on, guys, let's go back to the main house. The lovebirds need some alone time." A smile tugged on her lips. "Congrats, Doc. I knew you were smarter than you look."

As the three Coltons drifted off, Derek turned to Chloe. "You sure you want to marry into this family?" he teased.

"Positive," she said. She stood on her tiptoes and kissed him again. "In fact, when it comes to you, Derek Colton, I've never been more sure of anything in my life."

Epilogue

The motel was located on the outskirts of the city, an L-shaped building with a ramshackle exterior. Tate parked the Escalade on the gravel space in front of room eight. The top-of-the-line SUV was just one of the many toys at Ted Conrad's disposal—Tate's new persona definitely had some perks, though he did feel completely out of sorts in the tailored Armani suit, Gucci loafers and Hermes tie he was wearing. Definitely designer overload, but he was supposed to be a wealthy businessman, so he had to dress the part.

He also felt unbelievably naked without his gun. Walking into this op without a weapon made him uneasy, but again, he had a part to play. These people were doing Ted Conrad a favor, allowing him to inspect the wares before he committed to a purchase. He doubted they'd appreciate their customer showing up armed and potentially killing them.

Taking a breath, Tate got out of the car and approached the motel room door. It was bloodred, the paint chipped and the wood splintered.

The door swung open before he could knock. Tate found himself staring into the hard, suspicious eyes of a tall African-American man with a shaved head.

"Conrad?" the man barked.

Tate nodded.

"Got ID?"

With another nod Tate reached into the inner pocket of his jacket and removed an expensive leather wallet. He extracted his brand-new driver's license and handed it over.

The bulky man studied the license for several long minutes before handing it back. He opened the door an inch wider, then peered beyond Tate's shoulders and studied the parking lot. "You alone?"

"Yes, just like you ordered."

The door opened another inch. "Come in."

Tate was surprised by how easy that was, but he suspected the players in the ring had already vetted the hell out of his recently acquired identity. Besides, the entire time he'd stood on that stoop, he'd felt eyes burning into his back, which told him the entire motel was being watched and every arrival was being observed.

As he followed the beefy man into the room, the scent of mildew, pine cleaner and urine filled his nostrils. Tate wrinkled his nose, about to make some haughty, rich-person complaint, when his gaze landed on the bed.

And his breath caught in his lungs.

It took every iota of willpower not to react to the sight before him.

Three young women were huddled on the bed, donning blank, glassy expressions that hinted of the drugs coursing through their systems. All three wore slinky white nightgowns, the kind you saw in those tawdry boudoir portraits or really cheesy pornos. Two of the girls had dark hair and brown eyes.

The third was a redhead.

Agony burned a path up Tate's spine.

He tried not to show too much interest in any one girl, but his gaze kept returning to the redhead. Focusing on those big, blue-gray eyes. The angelic features. The perfect alabaster skin.

Hannah Troyer.

God, she was here. She was alive.

"You can touch if you'd like."

Tate swiveled his head in time to see a second man step ou of the bathroom to the right. Also boasting a shaved head, thi man had olive-toned skin, a bushy goatee and a leer on his face

"Give those asses a squeeze," Goatee Man offered, wigglin; his eyebrows. "Fondle a breast or two."

Tate almost gagged. Choking down his revulsion, he paste(on a cool, indifferent look. "I've seen all I need to see."

Tearing his gaze off the woman who'd been haunting hi dreams for weeks now, he moved back toward the door. "Tel your employer I'll be in touch," he said brusquely.

Without a backward glance, he left the motel room and gc back into the Escalade. His hands were steady as he drove ou of the lot, his breathing regular as he made his way down th dark one-lane road, his heartbeat steady as he put distance be tween himself and the motel.

It wasn't until he reached a stop sign that he unraveled lik an old sweater. Hands shaking, breaths ragged, pulse off-kilte

Gasping for breath, Tate rested his head on the steerin; wheel, resisting the urge to turn around, drive back to tha room, carry those sweet, victimized girls away and then retur to murder the bastards who'd dared to touch them.

Not yet.

He let out a shaky breath. Right, not yet. If he tipped hi hand now, he'd wouldn't be able to touch the ringleader. He' save three innocent girls. *Three.* Leaving the bastard at th head of this sex ring to hurt *dozens* of innocent girls.

I'm sorry, Hannah.

Choking down the acid coating his throat, he kept drivin; trying to erase the image of Hannah's big, empty eyes fro his head.

But he couldn't erase the rage burning a hole in his gut.

Or the all-consuming need to bring down every last bastar who'd dared to hurt Hannah Troyer and all the others like he

* * * * *

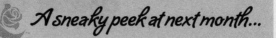

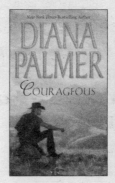